CHOICES OF THE HEART

RACHEL HANNA

FOREWORD

All January Cove books can be read in ANY order, so feel free to pick up any of the books in this series at any time.

I would also like to offer a FREE January Cove book to you as well! Just click on the image below to download your copy of WAITING FOR YOU.

CHAPTER 1

*P*aige stood on the balcony of the penthouse overlooking Manhattan and sighed. It was a beautiful place, but not where she necessarily thought she'd end up at this stage of her life. Her free spirit nature had led her here originally, but love had kept her here for the last six months.

She snuggled into the plush white bathrobe and eased back into the wrought iron chair as she sipped her coffee. It was bitter mixed with sweet, an irony that wasn't lost on her when she thought about her fiancé and his family. Bitter mixed with sweet.

She'd originally met Daniel Richmond, eventual heir to the Richmond real estate fortune, six months ago at a charitable event where she was serving appetizers. He'd caught her eye the moment he walked in, wearing his black Italian suit. She wasn't hung up on money or status; in fact, it turned her off most of the time. Instead, she'd noticed the kindness in his eyes and the sparkle of his perfect smile. She'd never seen teeth so white and straight in person.

He was flanked that evening by his mother and sister, both the epitome of snobbery. But not Daniel. He was grounded, happy and focused on what people were saying to him. Yet he kept looking at her. Smiling at her.

Once his family had left the event, he'd cornered her and started a conversation - at first, about the charity. But eventually, he'd gotten her number and promptly called her the next day.

The rest, as they say, is history.

And just last night, in the middle of Central Park, he'd dropped to one knee and proposed. She'd felt like she was in the middle of a fairytale, and she didn't want to wake up. Daniel was everything to her. He said all the right things, did all the right things. He was more than she ever thought she deserved.

But today was the day they were going to tell the good news to his mother, and she wasn't going to like it. Not one bit. She'd done everything in her power to make Paige feel like an outsider, like a "less than".

"Good morning," Daniel said, leaning down and kissing her on the top of her head.

"Good morning, my fiancé," she said, her smile gleaming in the morning sun. "I still can't believe I'm going to be Mrs. Paige Richmond soon."

Daniel smiled. "And I couldn't be happier, my love. We're going to do great things together."

Daniel had big plans, but they didn't involve real estate. Although he stood to inherit the family fortune, he was more interested in being a full-time philanthropist and starting his own charity. They were going to give to the poorest of the poor all over the world, and they planned to travel to Africa shortly after their honeymoon to put wells in ten different villages.

Her life was going to mean something because of Daniel.

Her upbringing hadn't been the best. Born and raised in a small Tennessee town, Paige had been abandoned by her teenage mother as an infant. She was bounced from one inadequate foster family to another until she ended up in the home of Ada Housley when she was thirteen years old.

Ada was an older woman in her seventies who

was known for taking in "problem children", and Paige was definitely classified as one during her formative years. Ada had been patient and kind, but she was older and it was pretty embarrassing for Paige when she'd show up at school with her cane.

When Paige was seventeen and had just graduated from high school, Ada passed away and she was left alone once again. So, she decided to become a bit of a gypsy, moving from place to place, taking on odd jobs to make ends meet. She'd lived in seedy motels and occasionally under a bridge, but she had lived life on her own terms. And surprisingly, she was happy most of the time.

She had worked the oddest jobs during that period of her life. Singing on the street, though she couldn't carry a tune in a bucket. Working as a waitress at a zombie themed diner. Handing out goat food at a small petting zoo. But all of those weird and wacky jobs had sustained her for years on end as she made her way up the East coast.

After a few years, she'd ended up in New York City at the age of twenty-three. Tired of traveling and living on scraps, she'd found a job working with a catering company as a server at high end parties. It was a dream job for her because she'd never seen such luxury, although she went home to her roach-infested motel room for weeks until she could afford even the most modest apartment about forty-five minutes from the city.

Life hadn't been easy for Paige at all, but she took it in stride most of the time. She was proud of herself and how she'd somehow managed to survive with just the internal fortitude she had. And normally, she was full of confidence, but when it came to dealing with Daniel's mother, Madeline Richmond, she was like a puddle of goo on the floor.

She stumbled over her words and had no idea what to say. She stammered and stuttered and her hands would sweat profusely, not to mention the rivers of sweat rolling between her boobs. She worried that she'd start dripping onto the elegant marble floors in Madeline's home at some point soon.

Madeline had been rude to Paige over and over again, usually when Daniel wasn't in the room. But when he left to use the restroom or take a phone call, Madeline would make it quite clear that, in her eyes, Paige was not nearly good enough for her only son. And his money.

Daniel's father had died when he was a teenager,

and his intention was for his son to continue running his real estate empire with an iron fist just like he had. Madeline inherited everything upon his death, but she too planned for her son to take things over and soon. The fact that he hadn't done so yet was bothersome to Madeline as she really wanted to spend her days shopping and getting pampered instead of running a multi-million dollar real estate conglomerate.

And then there was his sister - Tori Richmond-Gallagher. She was tall, perfectly built by the most popular personal trainers money could buy - not to mention the plastic surgeons - and married to Hampton Gallagher. His family ran vineyards from California to Italy, and his money was more than enough for her although her father had left her a trust fund before his death that would make sure she was never without all of the trappings that immense wealth could buy.

Paige had mentioned his mother's dislike of her to Daniel many times, but Daniel had always said things like, "she'll come around" or "she's just hard to get to know", but it didn't seem like either of those comments were true.

"I just called my mother, and she's expecting us

for brunch in about an hour and a half," he said, sitting down in the chair across from her and holding her hand. "I can't wait to tell her our good news."

"Daniel, you realize your mother isn't going to be happy about this, right?"

"I think you're misjudging her, sweetie. She only wants me to be happy, and being with you makes me happy." He leaned in and kissed her softly on the lips, sending shivers up her body.

"You know if you kiss me, we're going to be late," she said with a giggle before jumping up and running into the apartment. Daniel following, laughing as he caught her and swung her around.

THEY PULLED into the driveway of the Richmond mansion a little after ten. Madeline wasn't going to be happy that her son was late for brunch, but Paige could hardly be upset about it. He was good at a lot of things, and this morning he'd shown her just how good he was yet again.

Six months was quick when it came to dating and marriage, but Paige was ready to settle down in her life and she knew Daniel was the one. She figured why wait when you know the person is your soulmate?

"Ready?" Daniel asked as they slowly walked up the brick staircase.

"Nope," Paige said, a nervous smile on her face. "But when has that ever stopped me from doing something?"

Daniel rang the bell, an odd thing to do at his own mother's house, but then his mother had weird requirements about a lot of things. Her butler - yes, an honest to God English butler named Edward - opened the door.

He wore a suit, not a tuxedo as most butlers had in the movies Paige had seen.

"Good morning, Mr. Richmond. Miss Emerson," he said with his regal sounding accent. "Glad you could join us." A stab of sarcasm, probably straight from Madeline Richmond herself.

He led them straight to the dining room where his mother and sister sat at the table. To his sister's right was her husband, Hampton. The trio looked at Paige and smiled, their faces hardly moving from the immense Botox.

"Good morning," Madeline said, standing and hugging her son. She ignored Paige and sat back down. Daniel pulled out Paige's chair and then sat down beside her.

"Good morning, everyone," Daniel said as the butler put a plate in front of him and Paige. There were wine glasses filled with orange juice as well as fresh croissants on the table.

"Daniel, it's proper etiquette to always be on time for your commitments, dear," his mother said. "I certainly hope you don't keep our clients waiting this way."

"Mother, we were less than ten minutes late," he said. The fact that he had to answer to his mother like a child made Paige crazy. Having never had a mother, though, she didn't know if she was just sensitive or if she was completely right.

"Hello, Paige," Madeline finally said, looking her way only briefly before she turned to her daughter. "Tori, your hair looks beautiful that way…"

And again, Paige felt woefully out of place. Mansions and fancy brunches were not her "thing", but she did them for Daniel. Her hope was that after they got married, he would break away from his mother's death grip and they could start a life together their own way.

"How's your omelet?" Daniel whispered to Paige.

"Very good," Paige said. "I just don't…"

"What's that, dear?" Madeline said loudly as she eavesdropped on their private conversation.

Paige looked up and cleared her throat. "I... I was just going to say that I don't like green peppers." Madeline glanced down at Paige's plate where she had segregated all of the green chunks to one side of her plate.

"Well, we'll make note of that for next time," Madeline said with a fake smile. "Or perhaps you could broaden your horizons."

"Mother..." Daniel warned.

"Hampton, I tasted your new wine last evening. It was a wonderful addition to dinner," she said, totally ignoring her son's comment.

"Everyone, I have an announcement to make," Daniel suddenly said. Paige reached under the table and dug her fingernails into his leg. He jolted and then grabbed her hand in his. Surely he didn't think *now* was the best time to tell everyone about their engagement. His mother was acting like a cornered rattlesnake at the moment.

Everyone around the table went silent, and Paige felt uncomfortable under their gaze.

"Yes, dear?" Madeline said, her syrupy sweet voice grating on Paige's last nerve.

"Well, we have some good news," Daniel said,

putting his arm around Paige as she looked up at him. "Last night, I proposed to Paige and she said yes. We're getting married!"

Then the world stopped spinning. Paige didn't know that silence could be so deafening. It was one of those moments where she could have literally heard a pin drop, and she kind of wanted to yank out her earring and toss it onto the floor to both test the theory and distract herself with the pain of a ripped earlobe.

"Excuse me... what?" Madeline finally breathed out, and Paige was unable to stop herself from looking at her mother-in-law-to-be. The woman looked positively dumbfounded, shocked and nauseous all at the same time.

And then there was his sister, Tori. She was frozen in place, a piece of her omelet dangling off the fork she held midair, her mouth gaping open.

"I said we're engaged, Mother. You should be smiling right now," Daniel prodded. Still, his mother and sister sat shellshocked.

"Congratulations, Daniel. And you too, Paige," Hampton finally said. Paige could tell he was just going through the motions and didn't really mean it, but someone had to break the thick smog of silence in the dining room.

"Would anyone like more orange juice?" Edward the butler said as he walked through the archway from the kitchen. Unaware of the current situation in the room, Edward had inadvertently allowed everyone to get their bearings as he nonchalantly walked around the table pouring more liquid into each glass.

"Daniel, may I speak with you privately please?" Madeline said, her lips pierced so tightly that Paige was sure her cheeks might split open at any minute. Daniel shot a glance at his fiancee with an apologetic smile and stood up, following her out of the room.

DANIEL STOOD across from his mother in the downstairs office and watched her pace back and forth for a moment before she came to stop in front of him again.

"Are you insane, Daniel?"

"Excuse me?"

"Look, I understand that men have needs…"

"Mother, stop! You're being crude," he said. "And this isn't about my 'manly needs'. I love Paige."

"Sweetheart, I know you think you love her. I get it. Once, back in college, I dated a boy who grew up on a farm. But I realized quickly that it couldn't work, and I married your father."

"Wow. What an amazing love story," Daniel said dryly, sitting down on the edge of the huge mahogany desk. "You should write poetry or something."

"Son, I want you to be happy. I truly do. And there's no way this girl will make you happy. You need someone who challenges you. Who complements you."

"And how do you know Paige isn't that woman? You barely know her, and you certainly haven't made any effort to get to know her."

"Daniel, she's a former homeless person with no family and no career. She's not worthy of..."

"Our fortune? Isn't that what this is all about, Mother? The money?"

Madeline jutted her chin out and looked down her long, slender nose at her son. "We are the most respected family on the East coast, and I won't have you marrying some degenerate gypsy."

"Enough!" Daniel shouted in a loud whisper. He stood and faced his mother once again. "Paige makes me happy, and I'm sorry you're not okay with that, but I won't be bullied into the life you want me to live."

Daniel started walking toward the door. "Think of your father, Daniel." He stopped and slowly turned back to her.

"What?"

"Your father worked his fingers to the bone building this company, and for what? If you don't take things over, it was all for naught."

"You can run the company. Or Tori. Or, I don't know, the board that runs it now can continue running it."

"He wanted his son to run it, Daniel. You know that. It was his dream. He wanted this company to grow and for you to be able to pass it on to your son one day."

"Okay, fine. Let's say that I decide to run the company. Why can't I do that with Paige by my side?" he asked, his arms crossed over his chest.

She took in a deep breath. "Because it's not right, and you know it. I won't have our good name smeared by your little..."

"Stop right there before you say something you can't take back," he said. "We're leaving."

He walked out of the room and down the hall toward the dining room, but he couldn't see Paige lurking in the shadows behind the door to the powder room. Oh, how she wished her hearing wasn't so good.

THE RIDE HOME WAS QUIET. Too quiet. She didn't know if Daniel was thinking through his options and deciding how to break off their engagement, or if he was thinking of driving them both off a cliff. But it was too quiet. And there weren't any nearby cliffs anyway.

"Are you going to talk?" she finally asked softly.

"I don't know what to say," he said, his piercing blue eyes staring straight ahead as they made their way through Manhattan traffic. As rich as he was, she never understood why he didn't have a personal driver.

"Look, Daniel, I would totally understand if you wanted to break off the engagement..." she started.

He jerked the car into the nearest open space on the side of the road, almost mowing down two pedestrians in the process and turned to her, his eyes fierce. He reached across the space between them and claimed her lips against his.

When he finally pulled back, she was breathless. "You listen to me, Paige Emerson. I will never give you up. Do you hear me? Never. Not for anyone. Not for anything."

She nodded her head and smiled, stunned by the ferocity of his words and his kiss. She'd never seen him like that, but right now all she could think about was getting back to the penthouse as quickly as possible… preferably while he was still in his alpha male mode. She wanted to try a few things…

CHAPTER 2

*P*aige stood in the empty reception hall, looking around at the available space.

"I think we can put the wine bar over here, but the wedding cake will probably have to go over there in the corner. Wait, where is the band setting up?" she asked her co-worker, Sandi.

The wedding they were working today was one of the biggest she'd been involved in. Of course, her upcoming wedding to Daniel would probably be the affair of the year in Manhattan, and that made her nervous and uncomfortable. If it were totally up to her, she would elope to a beach somewhere to say her vows. Without Madeline Richmond.

"So let me get this straight," Sandi said as they sat

down to take a break. "Your mother-in-law-to-be called you a gypsy?"

Paige laughed. "Yep. Nice, huh?"

"Yeah, she seems like a lovely woman. What are you going to do?" Sandi asked as she started folding the cloth napkins into swans.

"I'm not going to do anything... except marry her son."

"Seems like that's a death wish," Sandi said with a laugh.

"Maybe, but Daniel wants to marry me, and I want to marry him so she's just going to have to deal with it."

"She doesn't strike me as the type to just deal with things."

Paige walked across the room with a tape measure in her hand. "Do you think this corner is going to be big enough for the band?" she asked. And then she heard someone clear their throat behind her. She darted her eyes to Sandi who was frozen in place with her mouth hanging open and her eyes as big as saucers. "What?"

Paige slowly turned to find Madeline standing in the doorway, her lips pressed together so hard that it looked like her face might shatter into a million pieces.

She was dressed to the nines in her pale pink designer suit and stiletto heels. Her purse, which was worth more than two months of Paige's salary, was pulled tightly against her side like she'd just walked into a prison instead of a pretty nice banquet hall.

"I need to get something from my car," Sandi said, rushing toward the door. Sandi didn't own a car.

"Hello, Paige," Madeline said without smiling. "I think we need to talk."

Paige nodded, still without speaking, and walked to the same two chairs that she and Sandi were just sitting in. Madeline looked at the plastic folding chairs, sighed audibly and finally sat down, still holding her purse against her.

"I understand from my son that you overheard our conversation the other day."

"I did." Could she be about to apologize?

"You know, eavesdropping is not acceptable, don't you?" she said. Paige wanted to slap her across the face, but thought better of it.

"It wasn't intentional," Paige said shortly.

"Well, that's neither here nor there," Madeline said. "I came here to settle this issue once and for all."

"Issue?"

"Your desire to marry my son."

"He wants to marry me too, Mrs. Richmond."

"He's confused. He's young and men have needs…"

"Yes, I heard all about those needs during your conversation," Paige said, trying not to giggle as she stood up. "And I fulfill those needs quite well." Oops. Why had she added that little part?

Madeline huffed as she sprang to her feet. "You really have no couth."

"Couth?"

"It means culture. Manners. Refinement."

"Yes, I know what couth means. I just don't know anyone who still uses that word," Paige said, her feisty side finally making an appearance. "Look, Mrs. Richmond, or shall I say 'Mom'…"

"No. You shall not."

"I have a job to do here, and unlike you, I'm not able to snuggle up with bags of cash at night. So, can you please get to your point?"

"Well, your insult was a nice segue into my point. You seem fixated on my cash, so let's talk about how much it will take to get you on your way again."

"Excuse me?" Paige said, incredulous.

"How much will it take for you to get out of my

son's life and break off this silly engagement? Ten thousand? Fifty thousand?"

Paige couldn't believe what she was hearing. Her mouth flopped open as she stared at the woman in disbelief.

"Are you serious?"

"I'm willing to go higher if needed."

"You *are* serious. Oh my God." Paige turned and walked toward the window, her fingers sliding through her hair in frustration.

"Okay, maybe you need more. One hundred thousand?"

She turned to face Madeline. "Get out."

"What?"

"I said get out of here." Paige had lived on the streets long enough to know how to be tough, and right now she was as tough as she'd ever been, holding her balled up fist by her side.

"Not until you tell me what it will take to get you out of our lives... for good."

Paige walked toward Madeline and came almost nose to nose with her. "Now you listen to me," she said through gritted teeth. "I love your son and he loves me, and no amount of money will ever keep me from him. Do you understand me? I don't care who you are or how much money you have. As long as Daniel wants to be with me, there is nothing you can do to stop that."

Madeline took a step back, her expression impassable and then smirked. "My dear, you have no idea what lengths I will go to in order to protect my son. You've made a grievous mistake here."

And with that she walked out and left Paige standing there, sweat seeping from her hands yet again. She had a sick feeling in her stomach.

PAIGE STARED out the plate glass window in Daniel's penthouse watching the gray sky produce its first droplets of rain. The sky was getting darker as evening set in, and her mood was going with it.

She hadn't told Daniel about the confrontation with his mother, and maybe she should have. But she didn't want to cause him more stress, and it would only put him in the middle. For now, her plan was to just deal with Madeline herself. Maybe that would be her wedding gift to her new husband.

"You okay, sweetie?" he asked as he came up behind her, sliding his hands around her waist and nuzzling her neck.

"I'm fine. Just a long day."

"Oh, that's right. The Waverly wedding?"

"Yes. We were doing some preliminary setup, but tomorrow is the big day. They're a great couple," she said with a smile.

"Did it get you excited about our big day?" he asked, twirling her around to face him. She stared up into his gorgeous blue eyes.

"Of course. I can't wait to plan our dream wedding, Daniel. But more than that, I just want to be married to you. I don't care if we run off to Vegas," she said, a hint of hope in her voice.

He laughed. "My mother would kill me if I didn't have a big wedding. She'll want to invite the whole city."

Paige sighed and then faked a smile. "Of course. I was just giving you the option."

"So," he said between the kisses he was planting on her cheek over and over, "have you thought of a date yet?"

"Actually, I have been thinking about that," she said. What do you think about Valentine's Day?"

"Hmmm, kind of a cliche, don't you think?" Daniel asked with a chuckle. Paige stiffened.

"Sorry, I just…"

"Honey, I was just joking," he said with a smile, only she didn't think he was joking.

"It probably is silly…"

"No. It's not. If you want to get married on Valentine's Day, that's what we'll do. I'll hire Cupid himself to fly in and marry us if that's what you want."

She knew that he was being funny, but tonight just wasn't the night. He had no idea what his mother had done to her today. But she wasn't going to be the one to wreck his relationship with his mother, and if he knew that she tried to pay her to break up, he would've blown up his whole life and future over it.

So she was silent.

"Glass of wine?" she said, trying to change the subject away from the wedding temporarily. He nodded and walked into the kitchen as she sat down at one of the chrome barstools in front of the marble topped breakfast bar. He poured her a glass of white wine and slid it in front of her.

"Oh, that reminds me. Hamp asked me to meet him at the new wine bar tomorrow."

"The one in Manhasset?" she asked.

"Yeah. I'm heading over there in the morning, so I should be back by lunchtime."

Hampton's family was well known for their wine

business and he was opening a new state-of-the-art wine bar just about an hour away from the city.

As much as Paige couldn't stomach Madeline or Tori, Hampton had actually been pleasant to her most of the time. He always spoke to her, tried to make her feel somewhat included. But she had no illusions that he wouldn't turn on her in a heartbeat because Tori ruled their home.

"You want to go?" Daniel asked as he sipped on a red wine.

"Can't. The Waverly wedding, remember?" she said with a smile, secretly happy that she had a legitimate excuse for why she couldn't go with him.

"Well," he said, leaning across the breakfast bar, "I will miss you, my soon-to-be-wife." He kissed her softly, and she moaned.

"Why don't you show me how much you'll miss me, Daniel Richmond?" she said, reaching across and pulling on his necktie.

"Hmmm… Let me see how many ways I can show you," he said as he walked around the bar and swept her up into his arms.

PAIGE AWOKE BRIEFLY the next morning to find Daniel kissing up and down her neck. It was still dark outside, the October mornings cold and crisp. She barely recalled him slipping out of bed, taking a shower and then kissing her one more time before leaving for his day with Hampton before she fell back into a deep sleep.

But now the bright morning sun had awakened her, piercing through the wood slats of his two-inch blinds. She could hear the sounds of the city, ever so faintly at the height of the penthouse.

It was eight o'clock, and the Waverly wedding was starting in a few hours. She needed to get up, have her requisite coffee and get moving soon or Sandi would surely start blowing up her phone.

As if on cue, she heard her phone ding. "Leave me alone. It's too early!" she yelled across the room as she poured water into the coffee pot.

Ding!

"I don't talk to anyone before nine!" she yelled playfully back at her phone.

Ding!

Ding!

Ding!

"What in the holy heck?" she finally mumbled to herself, wondering why Sandi was so insistent on talking to her. They were good enough friends that Sandi should know better. Don't contact Paige before nine.

She looked down at her phone and noticed six texts from her friend. Grumbling to herself, she rubbed the sleep from her eyes and started reading them.

Paige, have you watched the news this morning?

And then...

Paige, please call me. It's urgent.

And then...

It's about Daniel. He's... in bad shape. Please call me!

Paige suddenly felt like she couldn't breathe, and her hands were shaking so bad that she dropped her phone onto the tile floor, cracking the screen in the process.

Unable to read the rest of the messages through her shattered screen, she used voice commands to dial her friend.

"Paige! Thank God, you're safe!" Sandi said in tears.

"What are you talking about? Of course I'm safe. What's this about Daniel?" Paige leaned into the breakfast bar and steadied herself.

"You haven't watched the news?" Sandi asked, her voice trembling now.

"No. I haven't even looked at Facebook yet…"

"Oh, God, Paige. I'm so sorry, but Daniel has been in a very bad accident. Between here and Manhasset. It's all over the news. They don't know if he's going to make it…"

The world started spinning immediately. She thought she might vomit, and her vision was getting blurry.

"No… No… That can't be…" she said as she lowered herself onto the barstool.

"They airlifted him to New York Presbyterian, Paige. You should get down there. I'll handle Waverly on my own."

"Waverly? What?" she said, too stunned to remember the wedding she was helping with today. "Oh, the wedding… I need to call for a cab. He took the car…" Of course he took the car, she thought to herself. He was in a wreck.

She hung up with Sandi and started pacing the apartment, unable to figure out what to do. After a few moments of deep breathing, she was able to call for a cab and get herself dressed, but she felt like a zombie. It was the only way she could cope with the situation.

Just don't feel anything.

THE CAB PULLED up to the door of the ER and Paige jumped out like a gazelle, throwing money at the driver as she bolted from the car.

She ran through the doors and straight to the information desk.

"I'm Paige. Is Daniel here? Is he okay?" The woman behind the desk looked at her like she was insane.

"Excuse me?"

"Daniel Richmond. He's my fiance. He should be here..." She started pointing aimlessly around the room.

"Ma'am, I can't give you health information unless you're family."

"But I'm his fiancee!"

"I'm sorry, but unless you're legally married, I cannot release any information about his condition." The woman looked apologetic, but impassable. "Maybe his mother can help you," she said.

Paige felt sick as she turned to see Madeline standing a few feet away, her face puffy and red. She was looking in her compact mirror, applying concealer and some kind of eye cream. Paige wanted to lunge at her for being so vain during a time like this, but she knew that wouldn't get her in to see Daniel.

"Mrs. Richmond," she said walking closer. Madeline shot her a hateful glance.

"What are you doing here?" she seethed.

"Excuse me? Why wouldn't I be here? He's my fiance."

Madeline snorted. "You will never marry my son."

Paige saw Hampton approaching from behind Madeline and ran to him. "Hamp, how is he? Have you seen him?"

He looked at Madeline and then back to Paige. "I really don't know anything yet, Paige."

Madeline saw Tori coming back with coffee and walked to meet her daughter across the waiting area. Paige turned back to Hampton.

"Look, I can't say much because you're not…"

"Family? Come on. You know Daniel wouldn't agree." A tear rolled down her cheek. "I just need to know how he is."

"Fine," he said, pulling her around the corner out of sight. "He has major head injuries, Paige. Life threatening head injuries. Doctors aren't overly optimistic right now. They said the next twenty-four to forty-eight hours are critical, but he may never regain consciousness. Even if he does, he suffered a lot of damage..." Hampton's voice was shaking.

"Oh my God. No..." she said, falling into a sobbing mess against Hampton's tailored suit. He let her stay there, not touching her, until she pulled herself back together. "Can I see him? Can you sneak me in or something?" she begged.

"Paige, I can't. Madeline is watching everyone like a hawk. And I have to be honest with you. Her intention is to keep you from seeing him. And she has the power to do it as his next of kin."

Paige slid down onto a chair and cried. How could this be happening? How could this woman be so cruel?

"Hampton, you know he loves me."

"I know. Look, I can't rock the boat. And I've already told you too much as it is," he said. She looked up at him. "You should go home, Paige."

Home? Where was that? Daniel's penthouse? The streets?

Home was where Daniel was. Right now she had no home.

HER BACK WAS KILLING HER. She'd been sleeping in the waiting room chair for hours until Sandi woke her up. Confused, she stared up at her friend, who was still dressed in her catering attire. It was now dark outside, and a whole different cast of characters was sitting around her in the ER.

She didn't see Madeline or Tori or Hampton anywhere.

"Where are they?" she asked, shooting up from her seat, her hair askew and makeup running down her face.

"Paige, calm down," Sandi said, trying to get her to stop yelling and causing a scene. "Listen, honey, you need to come with me. You can't stay here like this."

"I can't leave. Daniel is here…" she sobbed.

"Sweetie, I know. But the hospital can't give you any information. It does no good for you to be here. I've come to take you home."

"What home?"

Sandi looked at her friend sympathetically. "You can come home with me. Or I can take you back to the penthouse. Or I can stay there with you. Whatever you want."

"I don't even know if he's still alive, Sandi. I need to know something."

"Look, we'll come back tomorrow when you've gotten some sleep and a nice hot shower. I'll help you, okay?"

Paige nodded and allowed her friend's arm to slide around her for support. Oh, how she wished it was Daniel's arm right now.

AFTER LEARNING from the news reports overnight that Daniel had been moved to ICU, Paige showed up at the hospital as soon as the sun was up. She'd had a fitful night of sleep at the penthouse. Sandi had stayed over, and the two of them had piled up on the plush sectional sofa because Paige just couldn't bring herself to sleep in their bed alone.

She walked to the front desk, this time as calmly as possible, and waited for the woman to look up.

"Can I help you?"

"Yes, please. My fiance, Daniel Richmond, is here in ICU. I'd like to get an update on his condition. Please."

The woman crinkled up her nose. "I'm sorry, but due to privacy laws…"

"I know you can't give me specifics, but can you tell me something? Anything?" Paige pleaded.

The woman smiled sadly. "No. I'm so sorry. I could lose my job. Mr. Richmond's information is completely locked down. The privacy level is very high," she said, barely above a whisper. Madeline Richmond had huge power in the area. No doubt she'd put the lockdown in place.

She really did look apologetic, but Paige felt stuck. What was she going to do? She turned back to Sandi and saw Tori walking through the double doors from the outside with several Starbucks cups in a drink carrier. She ran to her.

"Tori, thank goodness! How's Daniel?" she asked.

Tori turned and looked at her, the same snooty expression as her mother's spreading across her face.

"Why are you here?" she asked.

"Why wouldn't I be here? I'm Daniel's fiancee."

Tori laughed without smiling. "Listen, Paige, that time of your life is over. My brother is fighting for his life, quite literally, and you're a distraction here. If you come back to this hospital, I'll have the police called. You're not wanted here." She started walking again. Paige grabbed her arm, causing coffee to spill through the hole at the top of one of the cups. Tori snarled at her.

"I love your brother, Tori. And he loves me. If he hears my voice…"

"It's not going to happen. You can sit out here day after day until you're old and gray. My mother will protect my brother, and she will never allow you to see him."

"Why do you guys hate me so much?" Paige asked, tears streaming down her face.

Tori stared at her for a moment. "You need to leave."

Paige watched her walk through the double doors leading to the ICU waiting area and sobbed into Sandi's shoulder.

"You've got to eat something, Paige," Sandi urged, sitting across from her at the diner just down from the hospital. Sandi had ordered a sandwich for herself and forced Paige to order some soup, but she hadn't taken a bite in the thirty minutes it had been in front of her.

Instead, she stared out the large plate glass window onto the streets of Manhattan. She watched people walking, and rushing, through their days. She watched taxis speeding from one place to another. She watched mothers pushing their babies in strollers and tourists taking photos of random objects.

She just couldn't understand how the world was still turning while her precious Daniel was fighting for his next breath. Nothing made sense anymore.

"Paige?" Sandi called again. She turned to look at her friend, her expression dark and clouded by worry.

"What if he dies?"

"Don't say that. Look, you've got to eat something to keep your strength up…" she said, sliding the soup closer to Paige. Instead, Paige slammed her fist down onto the table, causing the other diners to turn and stare.

"Damn it! I don't want any freaking soup! I want Daniel!" she said before bursting into tears again. "What are you looking at?" she shouted at the people staring at her. Most of them turned back around, whispering to their table mates about the scene.

The cook behind the counter shot a glance to Sandi. She mouthed apologies and waved him off.

"What can I do for you?" she asked softly. Paige looked back and shook her head.

"I'm so sorry. I know you're only trying to help me." She reached across and held Sandi's hand. "I just don't know what to do next."

"You just take one more step, Paige. Just one

more step and then the next one. We'll do it together."

Sandi was the closest thing she would ever have to a sister, and right now she was the only person holding Paige together.

CHAPTER 3

*P*aige sat in the waiting room of the hospital, just like she had everyday for the last week. She didn't care about Tori's threat of calling the police. She had a right to sit there, and she would do it for as long as necessary.

No one would tell her anything, but as long as she saw family members still filtering in and out, she knew Daniel was still alive.

And as long as he was breathing, there was hope in her mind.

She hadn't worked in days, and she had barely eaten. She slept on the sofa of the penthouse and couldn't go into their bedroom yet. Everything reminded her of Daniel, and sometimes that was too much to take.

She missed his smile. His hugs. His warm kisses. She tried to hold on to the last kiss he'd given her in the wee hours of that morning, but each day the memory of the sleepy moment faded a little more.

"Hamp!" she called as she saw Tori's husband walking out of the double doors. He was walking toward her. Maybe he had news.

"Hey, Paige," he said softly.

"How's Daniel?" she asked, a hopeful smile on her face.

"You know I can't…"

"Please. I'm begging you." She held her breath.

"He's about the same. It's not looking good, Paige. You need to prepare yourself."

"No! I won't even think about that," she said, tears welling in her eyes. "God, I miss him so much…"

"We all do."

"Maybe if you can sneak me in. I know if he hears my voice, he'll wake up, Hamp…"

"Paige, no. Madeline would never allow it. Look, I was sent out here to… talk to you about something."

"What?" she asked confused.

"The penthouse."

She froze in place. The penthouse was Daniel's. She was only a guest.

"What about it?"

"Madeline is his power of attorney, Paige. And she wants you… out."

"She wants me out? While her son is fighting for his life, this is what she's worried about?" Paige said, bolting up out of her chair.

"It's her legal right."

Paige faced him. "You know she's wrong, Hampton. Why don't you man up and do the right thing and speak on behalf of your brother-in-law?"

Hampton stood silent. He took a deep breath and looked away. "The locksmith is coming by tomorrow at noon. You need to be gone by then."

With that, her only small link to Daniel was gone as she watched Hampton walk back through the double doors.

PAIGE SAT on Sandi's sofa and sighed. She was thankful to have a roof over her head, even if it wasn't a penthouse. Instead, it was a six-hundred square foot studio apartment in a questionable part of town with one of those kitchens where you could touch the walls on both sides at the same time. But now it was home… at least temporarily.

"That woman is the world's biggest witch," Sandi said, taking a sip of her wine.

"True story," Paige downed her third margarita. She was bordering on drunk, her petite frame not able to withstand the onslaught of so much alcohol at once. Sandi reached across the table and took her glass.

"You're done for awhile," she said. Paige slammed her forehead onto the table.

"Margaritas are the one good thing in my life right now, Sandi."

"That's not true. Everything is going to work out, Paige. You just have to hang on."

Paige looked up at her. Her face was a mess of mascara and tears, her eyelids red and puffy from nearly constant crying. And now her eyes were bloodshot on top of it.

"How is this ever going to work out? Let's look at the options. Number one, Daniel could die…"

"You shouldn't say that."

"It's true. That's what Hampton was trying to tell me. Number two," she said through slurred speech, "he could live but have brain damage. Or three, he could live and be totally fine, but I would still have to deal with his mother trying to keep us apart. There's no winning here." She was staring at her fingers wondering why they looked so blurry.

Sandi stood and walked behind Paige. She slid her arms around her neck from behind and hugged her.

PAIGE SPENT the next day sitting at the hospital again. She had to know what was happening with Daniel. But it was weird because she didn't see the family there at all. No Hampton. No Tori. No Madeline.

She waited for three hours before finally trying to get information out of the front desk lady. No such luck.

There was no other choice. She would have to go to the source. Madeline Richmond.

She drove to the Richmond building, hoping against hope that Madeline would be there. According to her staff, Madeline wasn't there and wouldn't be back for at least a couple of weeks. That seemed very odd given how entrenched she was in the business.

At that point, Paige felt she had no choice but to

go to the Richmond house. Thankfully, she'd watched Daniel put the numerical passcode into the keypad at the gate several times. It was a combination of his birthday and Tori's, so she easily remembered it.

She drove her compact car through the gate without incident and parked right in front of the house. As she knocked on the thick wooden door, she felt her palms start to sweat, her nerves getting the best of her.

Shockingly, Madeline opened the door. Her face was pale, her eyes puffy and red. She looked twenty years older, and Paige felt a twinge of sympathy. It soon passed.

"What do you want?" Paige noticed an almost empty glass of wine dangling from her fingertips, her hand hanging by her side.

"I want to know how Daniel is. Please, Mrs. Richmond. I need to know."

"Fine. Here's the update. He's dead." She slammed the door. Paige couldn't breathe. Her heart was pounding, her mind racing. Adrenaline took hold and she kicked the door so hard that it flew open. Madeline was walking toward the kitchen, and Paige wondered where Edward was for a moment.

"Don't lie to me! He can't be dead!"

Madeline turned, her bottom lip quivering. She dropped the now empty glass onto the hardwood floor, and Paige watched the glass shatter into a thousand pieces and fly all directions.

"My son is gone. Can't you just leave us in peace?" She was sobbing now, shaking visibly. In any other circumstance, with any other person, Paige would've reached out and comforted them. But not in this case. Not with this woman.

"I don't understand... I haven't heard anything on the news..." Realization was starting to set in, and Paige steadied herself against the wood and wrought iron bannister.

"We're keeping it quiet for now. He died early this morning."

"Why are you keeping it quiet?" Paige asked, unsure of why it mattered.

"Because we have a business, and this news could cause our stock..."

"Are you freaking serious right now?" Paige was livid. She wanted to strangle this woman. All she cared about was money and power and her standing in the community. It was sickening.

"Get out of my house." Madeline turned to walk away.

"When is his funeral?"

Madeline turned to face Paige one last time, and Paige could swear that her expression had changed to one of evil. "We're having a private family memorial. You're not invited."

Paige grabbed her arm. "You can't do that! He was my fiance. I loved him. Please... Please... If you have any decency at all, you'll let me say goodbye."

Madeline jerked her arm away. "We're done here. Don't come to my house again, or I'll have you arrested."

"You're an evil, evil woman."

"I've been called worse," Madeline said with a psychotic laugh. "Take some advice, my dear. You should move on with your life, maybe rent a trailer somewhere. Once you're back with your own kind of people, I'm sure you'll feel normal again."

"You stupid witch!" Paige said, lunging at her and just grabbing enough of her hair to pull out her extensions. Blond hair fell to the marble floor as Madeline shrieked. Edward finally appeared and pulled the two women apart before leading Paige to the door.

Minutes later, she was standing on the front porch alone. Totally and completely alone. The love of her life was gone. And she couldn't even say goodbye.

~

PAIGE AND SANDI stood at the edge of the water a few days later. Daniel had always loved the ocean, and this was the only place she could think of going to say goodbye.

She had already visited the site of his accident, which was almost too much to bear. She had cried so hard that Sandi had to almost carry her back to the car.

Since she wasn't going to get to go to a real funeral, she'd taken one of Daniel's old shirts and burned it so she'd have her own ashes to scatter. It was weird when she thought about it logically, but right now logic was pretty much out the window.

"I feel so lost," Paige said as she sat down at the water's edge, her feet being massaged by the lapping waves.

"I know you do, sweetie. I can't imagine how anyone could be as evil as that Richmond woman."

Paige sighed. She couldn't even cry anymore. She just stared straight ahead, her stomach nauseous from all the stress.

"I can't stay here, Sandi."

"What?"

"I have to leave the city."

"But why? You can stay with me as long as you want, Paige. I love having you there..."

Paige smiled at her friend and kissed her on the cheek. "You're the best friend I've ever had, and I appreciate it. But there are too many memories here. Everywhere I turn, I see Daniel. And I see the Richmond name. I just... can't..."

Sandi looked at her friend sadly. "I understand. But where will you go? And how will you pay for it?"

Paige turned back toward the ocean and took a deep breath. She raised her left hand up, allowing the bright sunlight to shine on her large engagement ring. It sparkled against her tan skin.

"Daniel gave me many gifts, but all I ever really wanted was his love. This ring was a token of his love, but it means nothing without him. I know he'd want me to use it for a fresh start."

"Oh, Paige... Are you sure you want to sell the ring?"

"I'm sure. Daniel would want this for me. I know he would. Plus, I'm going to donate some of it to his favorite charity. We were going to build wells in Africa..." A stray tear rolled down her cheek, and Sandi wiped it away like she had dozens of times in recent days.

"You're a good person, Paige. You deserve so much. I hope you find peace and love again."

Paige smiled sadly. "I doubt I'll ever find a love like this again. And honestly, I'm not sure I want to."

MADELINE SAT IN A CHAIR, her posture straight as an arrow like always. She took in a deep breath and sighed. She really hated not being on control, not knowing what was going to happen.

She looked at the small digital alarm clock on the nightstand beside the bed. It was after one in the morning, and she'd been sitting in this same position for hours now, but she was standing guard. She wouldn't let anything happen to him. She would protect him while he couldn't protect himself.

"Are you sure this was the right decision, Madeline?" her son-in-law, Hampton, said from behind her, breaking the silence.

She paused for a moment and then reached for Daniel's hand, holding it in her own. He felt so lifeless, so helpless. Her baby was her responsibility.

"Positive. As far as Paige Emerson is concerned, Daniel is dead." Her face was impassible, her jaw clenched.

"I don't think this is what Daniel would want…"

She turned swiftly and glared at him. "Go."

Hampton looked at the ground for a moment before turning and walking out of the small room at the rehabilitation clinic they'd moved Daniel to a few days earlier under the darkness of night and the protection of guards. He was being cared for by doctors and nurses who had all signed privacy agreements.

"I did this for you, my son. One day, you'll thank me."

PAIGE NEEDED a break from the constant crying and talking to Sandi about her feelings. She just need to get away and think about where she was going.

Her first stop was at the local pawn shop where she haggled for an hour before settling on a reasonable price for her ring. Normally, she wouldn't have resorted to selling her ring at a pawn shop, but she wanted to leave town as soon as possible and she had little in the way of savings.

The money she got from her ring would support her for several months, especially if she chose a modestly priced place to live. And that definitely wasn't New York City.

As she walked down the street, she looked up at all of the high-rises. The Richmond name was everywhere from banks to hotels to apartment buildings. And every time she saw the name - the name that was *supposed* to be hers - she felt a stabbing pain in her heart.

"Welcome to Carmichael's," the woman said as she walked into a small bookstore. It was a dying breed kind of bookstore, not like the big chains she most often went to when she wanted a book. This was a quaint place with dusty shelves and books crammed together, but it felt like a real bookstore. "Can I help you find something?"

"Well, I don't really know what I'm looking for, actually," Paige said, still feeling like she was walking around lost most of the time. "I'm about to move out of the city, and I'm looking for a... fresh start somewhere else. Far from here..."

"Ah, I see," the older woman said with an empathetic smile. "Too many memories here?"

"Something like that," Paige said, turning and looking around. "Do you have any travel books?"

"Sure. Follow me," the woman said as she led Paige up the stairs to the second floor of her narrow store. It was wedged between two large hotels like someone had found the one available tiny space in Manhattan and squished it in there.

Paige loved the smell of the tiny place. The paper, the lingering scent of coffee. It felt like it was a world away from the hustle and bustle of a big city.

"This shelf has all of our travel books and tourist guides. Thinking of going anywhere in particular?" the woman asked.

"Not really," Paige said, already starting to eye the wide variety of guidebooks. "I guess wherever the wind blows me."

"Sounds like my dream. I remember when I was back in high school, I had this plan that one day I'd be wealthy enough to close my eyes and point to anywhere on the globe and that was where I'd go. Of course, life happened and I never got to do it, but it was fun to think about." She smiled and walked back downstairs to help the next customer.

Paige stood there for a moment and then smiled for the first time in days. The thought of going somewhere brand new gave her a glimmer of hope that life could be good again. One day.

She walked to the small circular table in the corner of the room and found a globe. Beside it was a large laminated map of the United States rolled up.

She unrolled it across the dusty table and put two heavy books on each side to flatten it out.

Without hesitating, she closed her eyes and spun around a couple of times before turning back to face the map. Without looking, she shot her finger downward and touched the map.

Opening her eyes, she looked down to see where her new home would be.

January Cove, Georgia.

CHAPTER 4

*F*our *Months Later...*

Paige rang up the last customer of the day and flipped the open sign to closed. The longer she worked at The Cove, the more at home she felt. The small bookstore reminded her a lot of the one in New York where she'd first set out on her journey.

It had taken weeks for her to get to January Cove and get settled in. Wanting to save as much of her money as possible, she'd boarded a bus that took her to Savannah. She had sold her beat-up car back in New York and rolled that money into yet another beat-up car in Georgia when she arrived there, but January Cove was one of those towns where she rarely needed to drive.

Instead, she found herself walking most places or riding the bike she'd picked up at the local thrift store. Sometimes, in her darker moments when she was thinking about Daniel, she would remember standing in his penthouse looking out over the city and wondering how she managed to get there.

And then that life was gone in an instant.

Still, she had fallen in love with her new home and the few new friends she'd met along the way. For the first couple of weeks, she'd stayed at a beautiful B&B called Addy's Inn. There, she'd met the proprietors, Addison and Clay, and they were amazing people with a beautiful baby girl.

She'd also met Rebecca who ran the coffee shop called Jolt. She spent a lot of her off time there, enjoying some of the best coffee she'd ever tasted.

One of her favorite people she'd met was actually her boss. Her name was Elda Sue Myers, and she was about as old as the town itself.

Elda had run an ad for a store manager right around the time Paige had arrived in January Cove. She was an elderly woman, very frail and kind, and she had lived in the area for most of her life. In fact, her grandfather and father had run a large plantation near Savannah where she'd grown up and worked until she was married.

Paige was worried about Elda, though. Her memory was starting to fail her, and she'd kept her from falling more than once at the store. Elda refused to "stay home and rot", as she so eloquently put it. In her mid nineties, she refused to retire and came to The Cove most days.

All of the customers adored her, of course. She'd known many of the adults since they were babies themselves. Elda had never had children of her own and never married, instead considering the children of January Cove to be her own.

The closest relative she had was a great nephew in Colorado and maybe some distant cousins. Everyone she'd loved, including her sisters, had all passed away.

But Elda had taken her in as if she'd lived in January Cove her whole life too. She'd helped her learn how to cook some Southern meals, taught her about January Cove's history and shown her compassion at a time she needed it most.

It had only been four months. Four months since she lost Daniel. Four months and a few days since she'd last felt his touch, kissed his lips, shared the planet with him.

Getting over him was a work in progress; two steps forward and sometimes ten steps back.

For the first month, she allowed herself to cry through her morning shower and her evening bath. Then she'd cut it down to just her morning shower for the second month. Now, she didn't feel like crying anymore. Sometimes she worried that her tear ducts were dried up or that she needed to be treated for dehydration. Until Daniel had died, she never knew someone could cry that much and survive.

But she was surviving.

She was actually starting to look ahead. Renting a house was a big step, but she knew it was something she had to do. Living at the B&B for a few weeks had been nice, but she wanted her own space and now she had it. It had been a relief to learn she could afford the place without dipping into her savings and without getting a roommate.

The hardest part of losing Daniel had been not getting to say a proper goodbye. She'd always heard that funerals were for the living, and she'd found that to be so true in her case.

Having her own memorial with Sandi at the shore had helped a little, but she had just wanted to see Daniel one more time. She had no idea if he was cremated or buried, what songs were sung at his service or how many people showed up.

Madeline had said it was going to be private, and it must have been because Paige had scoured every square inch of Google looking for information without any luck. She had even called Sandi and made her confront Hampton at a wine tasting, asking him if Daniel was really gone.

Of course, Hampton had ushered Sandi into a hallway and looked at her as if she was crazy. Then he threatened to call the cops on her, and Sandi bolted.

Now, thousands of miles away, Paige had to let Daniel go. She couldn't change the past, but she could build a future, and that was what he would want for her.

"Knock knock," Elda said from the back office as she used her walker to maneuver herself to the front of the small bookstore. It was a cramped place, and Paige worried she would fall again.

"Miss Elda," she said, "what are you still doing here?"

"This is my home, sweetie."

"No. Your home is on Broad Street, and I'm taking you there right now." Paige smiled at her and then kissed her cheek.

She helped Elda to the door and turned off the lights behind them as she locked up. Most days, Elda walked the block to her home before dinnertime, but she'd stuck around tonight for some reason. Paige wasn't about to let her walk home in the dark alone, although January Cove had virtually no crime.

They pulled into her driveway, and Paige walked around to help Elda out of her small car.

"Come on, Miss Elda. I'll walk you to the door."

Elda reached up and took her hand as Paige opened up her walker. She wondered how long the old woman could continue living alone like this. Her hands were tiny, the thick blue veins covering most of her olive skin, a sure sign of her Cherokee Indian heritage.

As they neared the porch, Paige saw someone standing there. It was already dark out, the evening casting a dark shadow over Elda's porch.

"Stay here," she whispered to Elda, who nodded without saying a word. Paige reached into her purse and pulled out out her small handheld stun gun. She'd bought it when she first moved to New York, but she'd never had a chance to use it. Apparently, tonight was the night.

She walked quietly up the stairs and noticed the guy was turned toward the front window. He appeared to be trying to break in by the way he was leaned down looking through the glass. She quickly made note of his description. Dark hoodie pulled over his head. Dark wash jeans. Black boots. Once she shocked him, she would take a picture of him for the police, she decided.

As she walked up the last step, it creaked and caused him to startle. He turned quickly and took a step toward her, so she pushed the button on the stun gun and pressed it into his stomach. The jolt sent him backward, and he fell into the bushes off the other side of the porch.

"Ouch! What the heck?" he yelled, holding his stomach.

"Well, it serves you right for trying to rob an old woman!" she yelled back.

"What?"

"Oh dear," she heard Elda say from behind her. Elda was standing on the porch, somehow managing to get up the steps with her walker. Her hand was over her mouth and her eyes were as big as saucers.

"Miss Elda, stand back," Paige said, ready to tase him again if needed.

The guy started to climb his way out of the bushes.

"Stay back! I'm warning you…"

"Aunt Elda, help me out here!" the guy yelled, holding his hands up as he stood.

"*Aunt* Elda?" Paige was totally confused.

Elda chuckled softly. "Sorry, dear. This is my friend, Paige," she said to the man.

"This is your great nephew?"

"Yes. I'm sorry. I didn't know he was coming." Elda walked toward the front door and proceeded to unlock it while Paige just stood there stunned. Well, not as stunned as her great nephew seemed to be.

Elda walked into the house alone and started turning on the lights while Paige continued standing on the porch. She finally turned to the man who was rubbing his hand across his stomach where she'd hit him with the stun gun.

"Sorry about that," she mumbled. "But you really should've told her you were coming." She could barely see his face in the darkness, just the contour of it in the dim light of the porch lamp.

"I did," he whispered as he came closer. "She's known for a week now. We spoke on the phone twice."

Paige sighed. "Her memory is fading fast. I'm the manager of her bookstore, and I've noticed a lot of issues lately."

"Well, at least I don't have to worry about her

physical safety, I guess," he said. He wasn't laughing, though. Instead, he walked around her and into the house without another word.

"Goodnight, Miss Elda!" Paige called from the doorway as she turned to go back to her car, trying to get out of there as quickly as possible.

"Nonsense! Come inside for some coffee," Elda said, pulling her arm toward the house. If there was one thing Paige had learned while working at the bookstore, it was that you didn't say no to Elda.

Paige followed her inside and walked to the kitchen to start the pot of coffee. The old woman was great about inviting her in, but Paige knew she'd have to make the coffee herself.

She didn't see the mystery nephew once she walked into the house, but she could see light coming from under the bathroom door and assumed he was in there.

"Listen, Miss Elda, I'll start the coffee and head out. I'm really tired, and you need some time with your nephew…"

"Please stay. Just for a little while?"

Paige smiled and nodded, unable to say no to the woman who'd practically taken her in as a granddaughter these last couple of months.

"Okay, but just for a bit."

Elda turned to see her nephew coming into the kitchen. He'd removed the dark hoodie so Paige could see his face now, and the sight of him sent a warm tingle up her spine. He definitely didn't look like the ax murderer she'd envisioned on the porch.

He had sun tinged brown hair and a strong jawline with just a hint of stubble. His eyes were light colored - maybe blue - and he had the beginnings of laugh lines around his mouth. He was a rougher looking man than the ones she'd known in the city, or even in January Cove so far. His hands looked well used, and his jeans had faint mud stains on the knees. The black boots he wore were weathered and scuffed, and his arms were lean yet muscular.

"Hello?" she heard the guy say. Was he talking to her? She looked up at his face and he smirked. "My eyes are up here, by the way."

"What?" she said as Elda walked out of the kitchen toward her bedroom.

"I said my name is Brett. And you are?"

"Oh. Paige. Paige Emerson."

"Nice to meet you." He reached out to shake her hand, and she felt butterflies. What the heck? She reached out and took his hand, remembering to shake his hand with strength like she'd learned from Daniel. Show people you mean business.

"You've got quite the grip," he said, pulling his hand back and rubbing it as if she'd hurt him. And then she noticed his smile. Crooked, sexy, sarcastic.

"For a woman, you mean?"

He laughed as Elda walked back into the room. She hugged him tightly and then went up on her tip toes to kiss him on the cheek. She was a tiny, frail woman, and Brett towered above her with his broad chest and wide shoulders. He looked like a real life cowboy standing there, even without the requisite hat.

Paige could easily tell how much Elda loved him, and he definitely loved her too. His whole demeanor changed as soon as she entered the room.

"Isn't he handsome?" She reached one of her tiny hands up and rubbed his cheek. "Looks like his father."

"So how are you related exactly?" Paige asked, pulling three coffee mugs from the cabinet.

"My sister, Jean, and her husband had a son name Randy. Brett is Randy's son. And he has followed in his father's footsteps," she said, putting her arm around him.

"Oh yeah? How's that?" Paige poured the coffee

and slid it across the breakfast bar. Elda sat down at the kitchen table and Brett carried the cups there since it was easier for her to get in and out of those chairs than the high bar stools.

"He's a cowboy."

Paige almost spit out her coffee as she sat down. "A cowboy?"

Brett started laughing and rubbed Elda's hand. "I'm not a cowboy, Aunt Elda. I run a ranch."

"Same thing." She sipped her coffee like the Southern lady she was and smiled as she cut her eyes at Paige. What was she up to? "Paige, do you like cowboys?"

Oh. *That* was what she was up to.

"Miss Elda…"

"Aunt Elda…"

They looked at each other and laughed.

"She's real sly, huh?" Brett finally said.

"Can't blame me for trying. I'd like to see you settle down before I croak."

"Don't say stuff like that." Brett squeezed her hand.

"Thank you for the coffee, Miss Elda, but I really need to get home. I'll see you tomorrow?"

"Of course," Elda said.

"Nice to meet you, Brett. How long will you be

staying in January Cove?" she asked as she rose to walk to the door.

Elda and Brett looked at each other. "I'm here for good, actually," he said. "I was just out in Colorado for a few months helping a buddy get his ranch up and running."

"Oh. But I thought you have a ranch here also?"

"I've got people who run it now. My aunt needed me, so I'm here."

"I'm confused…"

"Oh, sweetie, I forgot to tell you. You know my memory isn't what it once was," Elda said with a sad smile. "Brett owns The Cove now. He's taking it over from me, so he's your new boss."

Paige felt her throat close up. Maybe it was time to find a new job.

BRETT LARSON HAD ALWAYS PRIDED himself on being a "man's man". Running a ranch had made him tough. His father wouldn't have accepted it any other way.

"You've gotta be tough, son," he'd say. "Nobody is going to give you anything in this world. You gotta earn it, you gotta keep it and you can't be a wimp."

God, he missed his father.

The two men had been close since the day Brett was born, but when fate had taken his life three years ago, Brett thought it would break him for good. He tried not to think about his father, but sometimes the memories came flooding back and paralyzed him for a few minutes.

Now, as he stood alone in The Cove, reorganizing the shelf of gardening books, he felt his masculinity slipping from his body. He could almost hear his father jabbing at him and laughing, and that thought made him smile.

"You like gardening?"

He turned to see Paige standing behind him, probably wondering why he was staring into space holding a book about organic gardening and grinning like a weirdo.

Brett cleared his throat and smiled. "Maybe I do." He slid the book back on the shelf and turned to face her. "I assume you have a key."

"I am the store manager, so yeah. Kind of important that I have a key."

She had a biting sarcastic wit, and he liked that about her. But even more frustrating was her beauty. She was petite but had some muscle in her arms and toned legs that he was noticing as she stood there in her short cotton red dress and black flats.

"My eyes are up here," she said, using his words against him from the night before. He looked at her and she laughed.

"Sorry. Aren't you cold? The air in this place feels like you could hang meat in here." Did she buy it? Or did she still think he was staring at her beautiful legs? Just for effect, he walked to the thermostat and messed with it.

"I'm from New York City, so this doesn't bother me. Trust me, once you've experienced a winter up there, this is a piece of cake." She walked behind the counter and pressed a button to open the cash register.

"New York, huh? I've never been there," he said, watching her as she counted the money from a small metal box and started loading it into the slots of the register. "You don't sound like a New Yorker."

She laughed and shook her head. "I'm not originally. I was actually raised in a little podunk Tennessee town, but life took me... places."

"Sounds like an interesting story."

"Not so much." She seemed guarded and wouldn't look him in the eyes.

"So what brought you all the way from New York to January Cove of all places?"

She turned and started fiddling with something on the shelf behind the checkout counter. He was obviously making her uncomfortable.

"Sorry, I didn't mean to pry…"

She turned back to him and smiled sadly. "No, it's okay. I just figured Miss Elda had already told you my story."

"No. Not yet anyway. I kind of want to ask her now."

Her eyes smiled at him, if that was even possible. They were blue with flicks of gray in them, and now his strong cowboy legs were feeling a little weak.

"No need to ask her. Short story is I was in love, got engaged and then my fiance was killed in a car accident. I came here to start over and get a break from the constant reminders."

His heart literally ached for her. She was a tough cookie, that much he could tell already. But underneath that tough exterior seemed to be a hurting woman, and he had always been a sucker for hurting women.

Not. This. Time.

He wasn't getting sucked in again. Every woman

he'd tried to save in the past had ended up shattering him. Not again.

"Sorry to hear about your loss," he said, repeating what his mother had told him to say as a boy. But he really was sorry for her loss.

"Thanks. Now, I'm sure you have some questions for me about the running of this place?" It was obvious that she didn't want to discuss her private life any more than he wanted to discuss his, so he was thankful when she gave him an out.

"Right, yes. My aunt hasn't really given me a lot to go on. I saw some of the financial spreadsheets, but everything looked like a mess."

"Between you and me, I met her tax guy a few weeks ago, and I don't think he's been looking out for her best interests."

"Taking advantage of an old woman?" She nodded, her eyebrow cocked up.

"I think so. He's from Hilton Head, so not a local. I stayed late one night and looked through the books, and I would swear the guy has been costing her money over the last few years."

She was smart. He liked that.

"We don't have time to go over the numbers right now since we need to open, but maybe we could chat after we close tonight?"

She swallowed hard and nodded her head quickly, obviously nervous for some reason. She cleared her throat. "Sure. Not a problem."

Brett leaned against the table to reach for one of the spreadsheets and flinched. His stomach was still hurting from her stun gun attack the night before.

"Are you okay?" she asked, looking at him as he rubbed his lower right side.

He smiled. "Yeah. Someone attacked me with a stun gun last night. It was weird."

Paige laughed and covered her face with her hands. "I'm so sorry about that. Did it leave a mark?"

Brett lifted the edge of his t-shirt revealing two small raised red marks. He was almost as stunned as the night before when she suddenly reached out and ran the tips of her fingers across the marks before pulling her hand back just as quickly.

"Sorry. Reflex," she said of her touching them.

"It's okay. I won't press charges for inappropriate touching... or for stunning me last night."

She laughed. He liked the sound of it. "Not a great way to meet, huh?"

"Not the best."

"Well, at least I can fix that," she said, standing up and holding out her hand. "Hi. I'm Paige Emerson. Nice to meet you."

He stood to face her, taking her petite hand in his and lightly squeezing it. Her grip was as tight as the night before, toughness being expressed in a simple handshake.

"Nice to meet you too, Paige Emerson."

And then she smiled again.

CHAPTER 5

*W*hy had she touched his abs?

The question rolled around in her head over and over all day. And now as she walked to Jolt on her lunch break, she continued mulling it over.

It had been months since Daniel had died. Maybe she was just longing for the touch of a man. After all, she and Daniel had been intimate regularly, and now she was in a self-imposed intimacy drought.

Falling in love with anyone was just too risky. Her heart had been broken, shattered really, into a million pieces. It wasn't worth it.

Still, why had she instinctively touched a stranger's abs?

And boy, they were nice abs. Cowboy abs. Six-

CHOICES OF THE HEART

pack, tanned, tight abs with those thick ridges usually reserved for serious bodybuilders. She had no idea that was hiding under his simple gray t-shirt, and she kind of wished she didn't know now.

"Good afternoon!" Rebecca called as she walked into Jolt. She'd met Rebecca on her first day in town when she was lost trying to find her way to the B&B.

Rebecca had seriously red hair and a fun personality from what Paige could tell. She was older, had a teenage son and dated one of the town's favorite sons, Jackson Parker.

The Parker family was known to be the foundation of the town, with five siblings and a strong widowed mother who had raised them all. From what she understood, all of the siblings lived in January Cove while the mother was traveling with her new husband.

"Hey, Rebecca," she said as she walked in. "Can I get my regular please?"

Rebecca smiled and nodded. "Coming right up."

Paige sat down at her favorite table, the one that gave the best view of the beach across the street, and sighed. January Cove was beautiful, like heaven on Earth, but she was still lonely.

Life had been hard for her. From her very earliest memories, life had been nothing but one struggle after the next. One loss after another. One disappointment after another. It was becoming harder and harder to trust that things would work out... one day.

The loneliest part was that no one really understood. Most people had parents, even if they didn't get along. She had no foundation, no stability. Daniel had been her rock, at least for the few months she'd known him, and now he was even gone.

Sometimes she let herself think about him. Although she tried to think of happy memories, Madeline's face often popped into the memory and ruined it like a wet blanket.

But as time passed, her memories were becoming cloudier and cloudier, like those moments late in the day when a person tries to remember their dreams from the night before. Parts and pieces. That's what she was remembering now.

She could no longer feel what it felt like to have his lips against hers. She couldn't taste his coffee-tinged breath. She couldn't smell his expensive cologne, although she'd gone to the local department store on more than one occasion trying to find it amongst the samples.

Gone were the feelings of his hand on her back, guiding her into a room. Or the sound of his heart

CHOICES OF THE HEART

beating against her ear as she laid her head on his chest at night when they watched TV.

He was fading away, and it killed her.

"How's your day going so far?" Rebecca asked as she slid a grilled cheese sandwich and iced coffee in front of Paige.

"Busy," Paige said. That was kind of a lie since the bookstore was anything but busy. She'd only seen about six customers the whole day so far.

"You looked a million miles away," Rebecca said with a knowing smile as she sat down across from her. Paige was starting to think of her as a big sister of sorts, but she really didn't know much about her. "You know, January Cove tends to be a safety net for a lot of people?"

"Oh yeah?" Paige took a bite of her sandwich and savored the richness of the butter and cheese, trying not to think about how it was clogging up her arteries.

"It seems like a lot of people end up here on their journey through life, and everyone has a story. I think you have a story."

"We all have a story, Rebecca," Paige said.

"Who did you lose?"

"What?"

"I know that look. Pain. Loss. Trying to reach back for those memories."

"Okay, what are you, a psychic?" Paige was fidgeting in her chair. "Mind reader?"

"No. Just a woman with a past full of loss."

"I'm sorry to hear that," Paige said.

"My husband died in the September eleventh attacks."

Paige's heart began to race. Anytime she thought about her beloved New York City going through that horrible event, it made her emotional. She hadn't lived there at the time, but she knew a lot of people who had lost loved ones.

"I moved here from New York City," Paige said softly. "I'm so sorry for your loss."

"Leo was just a baby at the time, so he really doesn't remember his father. And honestly, I struggle to remember things now."

"Doesn't that bother you?" Paige asked.

Rebecca bit both of her lips and then smiled. "Sometimes. It did at first. I can remember things we did together, big moments, ya know? But those little things like the way he hummed his favorite songs or the sound of him cheering on his favorite sports teams in the living room... I can't see them or hear them anymore. It's like they slipped away as time went on. And then Jackson came along."

"Did you feel guilty?"

"Very. I felt like I was betraying my love for my husband, but I wasn't. He would've wanted me to go on with life, to find love again. I know that much. I know he would've told me life was short and to move on, but it took time."

"Thanks for telling me your story," Paige said. Rebecca reached out and touched her hand.

"When and if you're ready to tell yours, I'm here. Okay?"

Paige nodded and smiled.

A WEEK PASSED BY, and Paige was getting used to her new boss. He seemed nice enough, but she hadn't spent a ton of time talking to him.

Elda had invited her over for dinner one evening, but the focus of the conversation had been on the business, and Brett seemed determined to get things in order for the bookstore.

Still, Paige couldn't deny that she was attracted to him. Thankfully, he didn't seem to share the same feelings which made it even easier to just stare at him when he wasn't looking. She wasn't ready for romance, not even close. Maybe she never would be.

She stood in front of the travel section at The Cove and stared at all of the books. Places she wanted to go, places she'd probably never see. Her one chance at being a jetsetter had been dashed the moment Daniel took his final breaths.

Not that she had loved him for his money. She wasn't a material person at all. She did love the freedom that money bought, though. She loved knowing that she was safe, even if it had meant occasionally seeing Madeline.

The thought of her made Paige's stomach churn. Maybe she needed some counseling.

She reached for one of the books with pictures of Greek Revival homes. She loved that style of home and the time period associated with it. As she was driving through Savannah on her way to January Cove, she'd seen such beautiful homes with the large moss-adorned oak trees lining the sidewalks. It was like a fairytale, and she hoped to take some time one day soon to do some sightseeing.

"Reading on the job?"

She whirled around to find Brett standing there holding a brown paper bag and wearing the whitest smile she'd ever seen. Dang, he was even better looking during the morning hours. She briefly imagined him just waking up, hair askew, the first hint of stubble peppering his jawline...

"Paige?"

"Oh. Sorry. You scared me."

"You don't seem scared..." Brett normally didn't come to the bookstore while she was working, so the shock of seeing him standing there made her breath catch in her throat for a moment.

"Well, I am."

"Hey, I'm not questioning you. I really wasn't trying to scare you. Where is that stun gun, by the way?"

"Very funny," she said as she walked past him and behind the counter. It was best to put some distance between them. Her body and mind were betraying her.

"Care for a snack?" he asked.

"What is it?"

"Only the best bagels in the world. Have you had breakfast?"

"No, I haven't, actually."

"Come on," he said, walking to the small back room. With the bell on the front door, they could hear any customers who might wander into the bookstore.

They sat down at the small table and Brett began to pull out the food. She noticed his well-worn hands. They were definitely the hands of a hard-working man, and they were so different from Daniel's. His hands had been the hands of a man who shuffled papers and got expensive manicures once a week.

"Cinnamon-raisin or blueberry?"

"Blueberry, please," she said. He slid a napkin in front of her and placed the bagel on it. "These are huge!"

"Yeah, they are kind of big." He smiled. Her stomach fluttered. "I got them at Al's. It's a little breakfast place over near Savannah."

"Isn't that pretty far?"

"Only about thirty minutes one-way, but they are so worth it. Here, try the homemade cream cheese."

She swiped the plastic knife across her bagel, slathering it with a mound of the cream cheese, and then took a bite. It was one of the best things she'd ever tasted, and that included all of those fancy restaurants Daniel had dragged her to in the city.

"Oh. My. God. This is heaven…"

Brett laughed, his dimples on full display. "Told ya."

"But I don't understand. You would've had to leave at six this morning to get there and back."

"I'm a cowboy, remember? We get up earlier than the sun."

"Cowboy, huh? I thought you said Elda was over exaggerating about that." She took another big bite of the bagel.

"Hey, I wear cowboy hats sometimes and cowboy boots most of the time. I own a farm. I train and board horses. I like plaid shirts and strong coffee and country music, so I guess I'll accept the title of cowboy."

Paige nodded. "Sounds like you've earned it."

Just then, the door dinged. Paige stood and walked to the counter.

"Good morning. Welcome to The Cove. Can I help you with something?"

The young woman smiled sadly. "I'm looking for books about Alzheimer's. I just found out my father has it."

Paige walked from behind the counter and touched the woman's shoulder. "I'm so sorry. You must be devastated. We have some books right over here."

She led the woman to the proper shelf and pulled a couple of books out. "I really like this one here.

There's a lot of information about the latest treatment options, and there are some other resources about the support you'll need as a caregiver as well."

"Oh, that sounds perfect."

"And make sure to call the local hospital. They have some support groups there and can also point you to any clinical trials that your father might qualify for."

"Wow. You're so helpful. Thank you!" the woman said. Paige rang her up and turned to walk back to her breakfast, but she found Brett standing in the doorway looking at her with a smile on his face.

"What?" she asked as the woman left.

"That was amazing."

"What was amazing? I just helped her find a book."

"No, you made her feel safe, Paige. You made her feel not so alone. You took time with her and didn't just rush her out or try to make a sale."

"I think you're over analyzing this," she said laughing as she walked past him and sat back down.

Brett rejoined her at the table. "You don't like compliments, do you?"

She thought for a moment. "They're hard for me, I guess."

"Why?"

"Who are you, Dr. Phil?" She finished the last bite of her bagel and stood up, walking to the refrigerator and pulling out her iced coffee from an early morning run to Jolt.

"Point taken." He stuffed the last bite of his bagel into his mouth and then tossed the napkin into the trashcan behind him. "So, I need a favor."

"A favor already? We just met a week ago."

He laughed and nodded his head. "True, but I'm still going to ask."

"Okay…"

"Well, you seem to be doing well managing this place for my aunt, and I need a little female perspective on something at my farm."

"At your farm? I'm sorry to say I don't know a thing about farming, Brett."

"Actually, I'm thinking of opening part of the property up for weddings and other events, but I need a woman's eye to see if it's even possible. I thought we'd stay there for the weekend."

Paige froze in place. Did he just ask her to take a trip to his farm and stay the weekend? She was torn between feeling excited and ticked off that he'd think she would just run off with her new boss for a weekend of raucous farm sex or something.

"Aunt Elda will be so glad to go back to Clover Lake."

"What?"

"My ranch is called Clover Lake."

"No. About Elda?"

Brett stared at her for a moment and then slapped his hand over his mouth before breaking into a deep laugh. "I'm so sorry, Paige. You must've thought I was propositioning you or something!"

"I... um..."

"I meant I was taking Aunt Elda to the ranch for a few days. I thought you could come along and give me some advice from a business woman's perspective." His eyes were filled with tears from laughing, but her stomach was in knots and she didn't really know why.

"Oh, thanks for clarifying that," she said, laughing nervously as she tried to play off the reason her face was bright red and her hands were sweaty.

"I know we just met, but you're doing such a great job for my aunt so I thought you'd be the perfect person to take a look. Plus, my aunt told me you did some event planning stuff in New York. And, of course, you're a woman of marrying age..."

"Marrying age?" She had almost made it to the altar...

"Jeez, I'm sticking my foot in my mouth so far I'll never get it out. Let me start over…"

Paige smiled. "Thanks for the invite, but I need to be here to run the store."

"Um, I'm your boss. Remember?"

"Are you forcing me to go then?"

"Of course not. But I've already talked to the temp agency and they're sending someone on a trial basis to take the load off you."

"I'm fine. Really. I love being here." She stood and walked to the front desk.

"Paige, I saw you looking at those travel books. My place is just outside of Savannah. I thought you might like to see some of those places in person. Plus, I'll pay you for the same hours you'd work here."

"You're a persistent guy, aren't you?" she said with a smile. She was seriously considering his offer. There was no doubt that she wanted to get away for a few days, and she definitely wanted to see Savannah and the area around it. And as long as Elda would be there… Funny that she thought a ninety-something year old woman was going to protect her and defend her virtue.

"Well?"

"Okay. Fine. I'll go."

Brett smiled broadly, clearly happy that he'd "won". She liked his smile. It was genuine and real, something she hadn't seen in a long time. Very few of the Richmond family had genuine smiles. Actually, only Daniel.

Daniel.

The thought of him caused her an indescribable pain deep in her stomach. Why did it feel like going on this short trip half an hour away was somehow cheating on him?

Maybe it was because Brett was attractive, and she was finding herself drawn to him sometimes. Maybe it was because those memories of Daniel were starting to fade. Everyday, she felt like she was losing little bits of him. His smell. His voice. The feel of his body entwined with hers on a lazy Saturday morning.

She was losing Daniel all over again, and it was just as painful as the first time.

"So, LET ME GET THIS STRAIGHT," Sandi said between sips of her Starbucks, "You're going on a trip with your hot new boss?"

Paige loved talking to her friend on the phone,

but they texted more often than not since Sandi had recently fallen in love with some wanna-be actor. She spent most of their conversations talking about Conrad - a strange name for a twenty-something - and his off-off Broadway production of what Paige could only surmise to be a story that mixed Hamlet with the zombie apocalypse.

"It's not like it sounds. He owns a ranch about thirty minutes away, and he's taking his ninety-something year old great aunt to spend a few days there. I'm just going along to give him some advice on using the ranch as an event venue."

"Uh huh..."

"What's that supposed to mean?"

"Come on, Paige. A woman has needs, and it sounds like a hot cowboy would be the perfect way to fulfill those needs."

"Sandi!" Paige said, turning around and looking behind her at Jolt to make sure no one was listening. She only had a few more minutes left on her lunch break, and Brett was watching the store in her absence until the temp could get properly trained. "I'm nowhere near ready for romance. With anyone, even a hot cowboy."

"So you admit that he's hot!"

"You're impossible."

"Look, Paige, it's been months since Daniel died. I know you're still grieving, but at some point you're going to have to move on and be open to new things." Paige knew her friend was right, but she'd never admit it out loud.

"Now is not the time. Daniel has barely been gone four months."

"Might I remind you that you hardly knew Daniel longer than that before you got engaged to him? I'm just saying that time keeps moving whether we like it or not, and you're going to have to allow Daniel to become a memory at some point. He's gone, Paige."

"I know," she said softly, taking in the words. *He's gone.*

"So when do you leave?"

"Friday morning."

"Are you nervous?"

"There's nothing to be nervous about. This is a business meeting, basically."

"Okay, sweetie. You keep thinking that. But if it were me, I wouldn't turn down a sexy cowboy who wanted to take me for a test ride…"

"Oh my gosh! I'm hanging up now, you nympho!" Paige could hear Sandi cackling with laughter as she ended the call. She couldn't help but laugh too, but it was more of a nervous laughter on her end.

After all, this was the first time she had been around a guy near her age in months. She'd purposely stayed away from men in general, opting to focus on rebuilding her life instead of finding new love. Daniel had burned a place in her heart, and she didn't believe there was much of a chance of anyone getting past the barriers she'd erected during the last few months.

But Brett was definitely handsome. And kind. And funny. And all of those facts meant she needed to keep her wits about her because she just couldn't - actually, wouldn't - risk her heart again.

CHAPTER 6

"Good morning!" Brett said as she swung open the door. She could see Elda sitting in the back seat of Brett's extended cab truck. It was big and black with shiny silver wheels and not a smudge anywhere on it that she could see.

"You're a little early," she said, her hair still damp from the shower.

"Sorry. Aunt Elda has been rushing me along all morning. You know how she is."

Paige nodded and laughed. "Yeah, she's always early. Give me a minute, and I'll be right out."

A few minutes later, she was out the door with her duffel bag in hand. Brett grabbed it from her and placed it in the back of the truck. Paige reached for the door handle to open it, but his hand covered hers quickly. She looked at him in confusion.

"In the South, a real man opens the door for a woman," he said with that sexy crooked grin of his.

"I can open my own door, Brett," she whispered, trying desperately to calm the crazed butterflies bouncing around in her empty stomach.

"I'm sure you can. But you're not going to." His eyes were piercing, but soft. Intense, but kind.

"Fine," she finally said, relenting to his need to be a true Southern gentleman. She climbed up into the seat, struggling to make it up there. For a moment, she wondered how in the world Brett had managed to get Elda into the truck in the first place. "Good morning, Miss Elda."

"Good morning, sweetie. Did you eat some breakfast?"

Elda was always worried that Paige wasn't eating enough, especially given her petite size. Paige had always been on the smaller side, although she was a full eight pounds at birth. But in her world, food had been scarce, so she wasn't ever overweight even slightly.

"No, ma'am. I sort of woke up late," Paige said with a smile as she turned and looked at the old woman. Elda barely fit the tiny seat she was sitting in, her frailty becoming more apparent each day.

"I made some muffins. Have one... Wait, have two," she said as she pulled two blueberry muffins from a bag beside her. Paige knew it would do no good to decline, so she took the muffins and thanked Elda before buckling into her seat.

"And off we go!" Brett said, a grin on his face. He backed out of the driveway and headed toward Savannah.

"You seem excited," Paige finally said as they drove through town. She tried to hide the fact that she was licking the blueberry remnants off of her fingers.

"I am excited. This is the first time I've had visitors at the ranch in awhile."

"Aw. That seems kinda sad." A sarcastic wit was one of the blessings Paige definitely had. She often wondered who she got that from - her birthmother or birthfather? Or maybe it was more of an environmental thing she'd picked up along the way. For all she knew, her birthparents were as dull as butter knives.

Brett chuckled. "Yeah, probably. I just don't get out much."

"Why's that?"

"I spend most of my time working. Not that I don't love running the ranch, but it can be a lonely existence. Horses only talk so much. That's why I took some time off to visit my friend in Colorado, at least until Aunt Elda said she needed me to come home."

Paige turned and noticed Elda already dozing in the back seat. "How many horses do you have?"

"Three of my own, but we board them too so we have about twelve right now."

"And you have a staff working the ranch?"

"Just four people. I have Randy who takes care of the horses. Phil handles most of the work around the ranch, fixing fences and stuff. Lou handles a lot of the financials, along with me, of course. And then there's Amira."

"Amira?"

"She's my... assistant."

The way he said it was odd, like he was trying to hide something. She decided not to dig further, but she was definitely interested in meeting Amira.

"I don't get why you decided to buy The Cove then. I mean, if you're so busy?"

"Well, Aunt Elda can't continue like this, and she

couldn't bear the thought of selling it to a stranger. So, I agreed to take it off her hands and see if I could help get it back on track, so to speak." He glanced quickly at his aunt, who had her mouth hanging open and was snoring slightly already. "Between you and me, it was really just to ease her mind, if that makes sense. I'm not sure The Cove is going to be a money maker or if I'll continue it on after…"

He didn't need to finish that sentence. And Paige could understand what he meant. Keeping a non-profitable business wasn't a good idea for anyone, but the fact that he'd done such a nice thing for Elda warmed her heart.

"You know, you don't look like a cowboy."

"Oh yeah?" He smiled at her and then looked back at the road. "And what does a cowboy look like?"

"Tight jeans, dirty boots, a big cowboy hat, outline of chewing tobacco in his back pocket, big mud-caked tires on his truck… Instead, you have hiking boots, a baseball cap and the cleanest truck I've ever been in."

"Oh no. They might revoke my membership in the Cowboy Club now."

Paige giggled. "I mean, can you really ride a horse?"

Brett looked at her, his eyes serious. "Oh, I'll show you just how good I ride when we get to Clover Lake."

Chills rose from her feet to her head, and Sandi's voice floated through her mind.

IT ONLY TOOK ABOUT forty minutes for them to arrive at Clover Lake, and Paige was astounded when they pulled down the long dirt road leading to the property. It was lined with huge moss-covered trees like something out of a Civil War era movie. Scenes from Gone With The Wind played in her head as the land suddenly opened up before them.

What stood before her looked more like a beautiful dollhouse than a real home. White with a sharp, peaked roofline, it was the most beautiful building she'd ever seen. The front porch spanned the whole face of the house, and over the doorway was a curved window with stained glass that made the home look almost church-like.

Paige could actually feel tears starting to sting her eyes, so she turned quickly to survey the land to the right of her. The property was magnificent, like something from a fairytale. The land was mostly flat with just enough of a hilly quality to allow her to see the back parts of it.

Horses dotted the pasture which was interspersed with those same mossy trees and pecan trees. Shade covered parts of the front yard, with the sun peeking through and creating a whole pattern across the the lawn.

"This is your home?" was all she could manage to breathe out. Never in her life had she seen something like this place, and she couldn't for the life of her figure out why Brett would ever leave. If she lived here, she would have someone do her grocery shopping for her just so she never had to leave.

Brett stopped the truck in front of the house and smiled. "This is my home."

Paige turned to make sure Elda was still sleeping. She was full-on snoring now.

"This is the most beautiful thing I've ever seen," Paige said softly as she continued to stare.

"I don't know if I'd agree with that," Brett said even softer. She had no idea what that meant, but by the time she looked at him, he was starting to get out of the truck. Before she could reach for her handle, there he was opening her door again. Maybe she could get used to this, after all.

Paige hopped to the ground and turned around slowly, taking in as much of the property as she could. It felt like her eyes weren't big enough to take it all in.

She turned to see Brett carefully lifting his aunt from her seat and placing her on the ground. Elda was smiling at him, her love for her nephew apparent. She looked at him like he was a superhero, and it occurred to Paige that he probably was in Elda's eyes.

"Welcome home, Aunt Elda," he said with a grin.

Elda looked at the home and closed her eyes as she took a deep breath. A smile spread across her face. "It feels good to be back."

"How long has it been?" Paige asked as Brett started gathering their bags.

"About a year." Brett said.

"Why so long?"

Elda spoke up. "Because even this short trip is tiring for me, my dear. But I couldn't wait any longer."

For some reason, the way that Elda said it concerned Paige, but she put that worry aside for the time being.

"Come on, let's get you both settled in." Brett

grabbed all of the bags himself and led them toward the front door as Paige helped Elda up the five stairs.

PAIGE STOOD at the window of the bedroom and stared out over the land. Her room was upstairs and looked over the horses grazing in the pasture behind the house. She had never ridden a horse, but she wanted to. Those Tennessee roots of hers were stirring in her gut with thoughts of her New York life seeming to fade more each day. Maybe she was a Southern girl at heart.

Her room was the epitome of Southern grace and old world charm. The large four-poster bed was covered in a handmade quilt, and thick moldings anchored the walls on top and bottom. There was white painted beadboard stretching halfway up the wall.

The hardwood floors were original, but gorgeous, and she had a rock-faced fireplace in her room - although it might be too warm to use it this time of year.

But it was the bathroom that had her mouth gaping open when Brett showed it to her. With a deep clawfoot tub, all she could imagine was sinking down into a warm bubblebath each night before sliding under the quilt and falling asleep to the sound of crickets chirping outside of her window.

This place was peace on Earth.

"Knock, knock."

She turned to see Brett's nose inching its way through the crack in her door. "Come in."

"Need anything?"

"No. Thank you. This place is just… I don't even have words."

"Want to take a tour?" he asked, smiling as he held up some keys.

"What are those?"

"I have a golf cart."

Paige laughed. Of course he did. This place was far too large to walk the land all the time.

"Sure. Let me get changed, and I'll meet you downstairs?"

Brett nodded and shut the door behind him.

WHEN SHE CAME WALKING down the front steps, he couldn't help but stare at her. She was the most adorable woman he'd ever seen, but she had a strength about her that most women didn't. From the short amount of time he'd spent around her, he knew a few things. She was sarcastic. She was private. She was hurt. She was still grieving. But she was special.

The spring air smelled of flowers. He had always loved that smell, although it often mixed with the aroma of horses and manure. She was wearing a pair of jeans, a pink T-shirt and sneakers, but she was still as beautiful as if she'd been in a cocktail dress.

He had to get his mind straight. Maybe he needed a good whiff of manure right now.

"So, what would you like to see first?" he asked.

She smiled. "I want to see it all. Can we start with the house itself?"

"Sure. This house was built in the late eighteen fifties by my great-great grandfather. He was a wealthy man and very well thought of in this area. It took years to build it, but he was involved in every step of the construction, right down to the moldings in the house."

"It's just a magical place, Brett. And you grew up here?" They continued to walk around the front of the house and over to one side.

"Yes. Most people in my family grew up here. In

fact, Aunt Elda's family had a house on this property when she was young, but it burnt down about fifteen years ago in a brush fire."

"Wow. That's so sad…"

"Want to see the stables?"

She nodded and they both hopped into the golf cart. As they drove over the grassy hills, Brett couldn't help but take the occasional glance at Paige. She was smiling and looking off in the distance, and it occurred to him that it was the first time he'd seen her look truly at peace. There was an easiness on her face that he hadn't seen before, and he felt pure happiness that he was the one who was able to give that to her.

But not looking at the path in front of a moving golf cart, even for a few seconds, can be a recipe for disaster. Brett turned to see the stump of a small tree that he knew was there - since he'd cut it down months ago - but had forgotten about for a moment.

When the golf cart hit the edge of the stump, it jerked to the side just enough to cause him to lose control and send them careening into a small patch of woods. When they hit a tree, the cart leaned and sent them both toppling out of the side.

Trying to keep her from hitting the ground, he

somehow managed to grab her as they fell out one side, which landed her squarely on top of him.

"Oh my God, are you okay?" he asked as soon as they landed in the crunchy patch of dead leaves.

"I'm... I'm fine," she said. He was lying on his back, his arms wrapped tightly around her waist. Her cheek was still planted against his chest. When she raised her head to look at him, their faces were almost touching, and he quickly realized she needed to be off his front side before she thought he was some kind of a pervert. In 3...2...1...

Brett shifted quickly, moving her to the side just enough to not be embarrassed at how his body was reacting to her being there. On top of him. He tried to conjure the smell of manure, but it wasn't working. She could've been covered in the stuff, and he would have hugged her anyway.

"Brett?" she said softly.

"Yes?" Was his voice shaking?

"I can't breathe."

He released her from his tight grip and helped her sit up. "I'm so sorry. I didn't mean to almost kill you."

Paige started laughing. "I guess we're even now. I've almost killed you with a taser, and you've almost killed me in a golf cart."

"In all fairness, both situations were your fault," he said without thinking as he stood up and reached a hand down to pull her up. She took his hand, sending an immediate shockwave through his body, and pulled herself up to standing.

"Excuse me? How were either of these situations my fault exactly?"

Now he'd done it. "Well... You tasered me."

"And you shouldn't have been lurking around on a dark porch..."

"Okay, fine. I'll accept half the responsibility for that one."

She put her hands on her curvy little hips and cocked her head to the side. "And how am I remotely responsible for this little mishap, Mr. Larson?"

Why did her calling him "Mr. Larson" make him want to push her up against a tree and kiss her?

Honesty. He was going to try honesty.

"Because I couldn't stop looking at you, and it distracted me."

She shifted uncomfortably and cleared her throat. She stopped looking at him, opting instead to stare off in the distance.

"You were looking at me? Why?"

"Because you looked so... peaceful." He wanted to say beautiful. Sexy. Drop-dead gorgeous. But he said peaceful instead. Mainly because he didn't want to scare her, but also because he was scaring himself.

"I did?" Oh good. She was making eye contact with him again. Maybe he didn't totally scare her off.

"Yeah. It was nice to see. You always look a little serious, but for those few moments - actually, since you've gotten to Clover Lake - you looked serene. Happy."

"Huh…" she murmured to herself.

"Until I crashed you into a tree, that is. I'm so sorry, Paige. Are you sure nothing is hurt?" He instinctively reached out and touched her arm, but she jolted as if his hand was burning her. He pulled back.

"I'm fine. Really. But does this mean our tour is over?" She was smiling. Smiling was good.

"No. Actually, we can at least walk to the stables from here. Do you like horses?"

"I want to like horses," she said with a laugh.

"You want to?"

"I've never even touched a horse, but I'd love to learn to ride."

"How about we start with touching one?" he said. "Come on."

As they walked toward the barn, he watched her looking around in amazement, but he also paid better attention to where he was walking. Tripping over a stump would be a bad idea at this point.

"Hey, Phil!" he called out to his farm handyman who was fiddling with a broken piece of fencing at the corner of the property.

"Hey, man! I didn't know you were home for the weekend 'til I saw Miss Elda watching her shows in the sitting room," he said, referring to Elda's lifelong obsession with soap operas. Her hearing was so bad that she had to turn on closed captioning now, but woe be to the person who interrupted her soaps.

Brett shook Phil's hand. Phil had been working at the farm for about a decade now, and he could fix anything - like some kind of mechanical wizard.

"Yeah, she wanted to come back for a few days. Phil, this is Paige Emerson. She's Aunt Elda's book-store manager. Well, I guess she's my manager now..." Why was he stammering? He was *her* boss, yet he was the nervous one.

"Nice to meet ya, Paige. Welcome to Clover Lake."

"Thank you," she said, reaching out and shaking Phil's orange clay stained hand.

"Listen, we had a little mishap with the golf cart over there in the wood patch. You think you can work some of your magic?"

Phil laughed. "How many times are you gonna wreck that thing, man?" He shook his head as he started walking toward the woods. Paige looked at him and bit her lips to stop from laughing.

"I'm not saying a word…" she said, giggling under her breath.

CHAPTER 7

*P*aige stood watching Brett as he checked on each horse in the stable. It was a state-of-the-art place with plenty of stalls and lighting. She was surprised at how clean it was, but Brett didn't seem to do anything halfway. Everything was top of the line, right down to his truck.

"Come here," he said, waving her over. She slowly walked toward him as he stood next to one of the horses inside the stall. It was a beautiful brown horse with a white stripe down its nose. "This is Noelle, my prized girl."

Paige reached out and rubbed her hand across Noelle's snout. The horse threw her head a bit, but calmed right back down.

"She likes you," he said softly.

"And how do you know that?" Paige asked as she continued moving her hand up and down the horse's snout.

"Because she tossed her head a bit when you touched her. That's how she shows excitement."

"How long have you had her?"

"About six years now. She was born on Christmas morning."

"Hence the name Noelle…"

"Yes, ma'am."

She loved how he talked. After living in New York City for awhile, she'd grown accustomed to the thick accents she heard on a daily basis, but it was nice to hear a true Southern accent again. For some reason, being called "ma'am" by Brett didn't make her cringe. It kind of made her legs feel weak.

"You want to ride her?" he asked, his eyes glimmered like a kid on Christmas morning.

"Are you serious? No way…"

"It's no big deal. I'll help you."

"But what if she takes off?"

"Noelle's a good girl. She won't take off."

Without thinking, Paige made a different suggestion. "I'll only do it if you'll ride with me."

"Of course. I have another horse I can ride…"

"No. I mean both of us on Noelle. Is that possible?" Why was she asking him this? The last thing she needed was to have her body pressed against his yet again. That golf cart incident almost sent her over the edge the last time. Who knew being thrown from a vehicle after hitting a tree could be so erotically charged?

"Sure. We can do that."

She could swear she heard his voice shaking.

Brett opened the stall and took Noelle out into an open area. Paige knew nothing about horses, but she watched him saddle her up and do all of the regular "horse stuff" that people must do when they want to ride. All she could look at was Brett in his form hugging "man jeans", a thin line of sweat on the back of his t-shirt leading to places she could only imagine.

There was something about watching a man in his element, doing things with such authority. Watching Daniel do his job had been different. There was nothing sensual about business phone calls and deals across conference tables. But watching a cowboy get a horse ready to ride was better than any romance movie she'd seen on the big screen.

"Ready?" he asked. Her face was flush with just

how much she was ready, and because of the fact that he just caught her checking him out.

"Yep," she said, slowly walking toward him.

"Okay. You're going to put your left foot here in this stirrup," he started to explain. "Once you do, push up and swing your right leg over Noelle..."

"Alright," she said as she started to do what he was telling her. She tried to swing her right leg over, but her petite frame wasn't allowing her legs to reach far enough. That's when she felt Brett's large hand on her butt, pushing her upward so she could get her leg to the other side.

When he let go, she felt the absence of his hand on her butt. What the heck? Why was her body betraying her and acting this way. She had just met him. And he was her new boss. And she was still grieving Daniel.

Before she had more time to think, he was swinging his leg over the horse behind her, and now she was nestled snugly between his strong, muscled legs. She could feel his taut chest behind her, the heat of his body mixing with the heat of hers.

"Ready?" he whispered into her ear, his voice a mixture of masculinity and Southern charm with a bit of gruffness thrown in.

"Brett! Brett!" she could hear a woman with an

accent calling in the distance. She turned to see what could only be described as a supermodel in a white sundress and cowboy boots running toward them holding a piece of paper. The woman had long, thick, flowing black hair with perfect waves. Her toothy white smile was on full display, and her ice blue eyes looked both beautiful and evil at the same time.

"Amira, what do you want? We're about to go for a ride," he said.

Amira. His assistant. The one he'd mentioned in the truck, and the very same one he sounded so unsure or evasive about when he mentioned her.

"Hello. I'm Amira. And you are?" She was looking up, directly into Paige's eyes.

"This is Paige. She runs the bookstore I just bought. Now, what do you want?"

"Is that any way to speak to your business partner, Brett? And in front of company…"

Paige could feel a lump forming in her throat. Business partner? Brett had referred to her as his assistant. She felt him shift behind her.

"Sounds like you two need to have a chat about your business," Paige said as she made a move to slide off the horse. Brett reached an arm around her waist and pulled her back between his legs.

"No. We don't. Amira can wait. I took today off," he said. His voice was stern as he looked at her standing on the ground. She was not happy. Paige could tell that much for certain.

"It's about the horse show."

"Which is in three weeks. We'll talk Monday. Have a good weekend," he said, and with that, he shook the reins and the horse trotted away, leaving Amira standing there. Paige couldn't help but take a glance back at her as they turned, and Amira looked like she could shoot daggers at the pair of them with just her eyes.

They rode in silence for a few moments, Paige enjoying the feeling of the gentle spring breeze against her face. She'd have been lying if she said she wasn't also enjoying the feeling of being against a man again, even if it was her new boss.

A part of her wondered if this was somehow inappropriate all the way around. Riding between the strong legs of her cowboy boss just a few of days after meeting him. And stunning him with her taser. Yeah, there was nothing particularly "right" about the whole situation.

And she was a strong woman with a good head on her shoulders. She knew when to stop, when to not let her emotions get the better of her.

"I guess you're wondering what that was all about," Brett finally said after riding for a few minutes. She could feel the lingering irritation in his voice.

"Nope. That's your business. I'm just the manager of a bookstore, Mr. Larson."

"Oh really?" he said with a laugh. "Well, I'm going to tell you anyway."

They rode to a spot beside a small pond and he stopped the horse. The place was beautiful with a newish dock and a gazebo beside the bluish-green water. Brett jumped off the horse and reached up, taking Paige's hand as she carefully started to slide off. Without warning, he picked her up and put her on the ground in one swift movement.

"I could've done it myself, you know."

"Yeah. I know," he said, smiling that dimpled grin that encouraged her to make bad decisions.

He led her to the dock, and they both sat down with their feet dangling over the edge. The water level was down a bit, so her toes were a good six inches from touching the surface.

"Amira is complicated."

Paige chuckled. "Yes, she seems to be."

In fact, Amira reminded her of a lot of the socialite women she'd met while working in New

York. High maintenance. Thought they were above everyone else. And yet she had to wonder why and how a woman like this ended up on a Georgia ranch.

"Her father was an investor in this place when my Dad was alive. We went through a rough patch back in the eighties, and her father became a partner. They were new to the US from Egypt. Amira was just a girl. We played together a lot when her father would come to look at the financials and keep watch over his investment. After some time, my Dad really didn't like him as a partner. He wanted to be a solo show again, but Ali - that was her father - didn't want to sell his share. There was a lot of contempt there. My Dad was so stressed over that and other things going on in his life at the time, he... well, he made a bad decision."

"Bad decision?"

"He jumped from a bridge, Paige."

Her heart clenched up. She wanted to reach out and hold his hand or hug him or something. She knew that kind of pain. Actually, his pain was probably a lot worse than hers. As much as she loved Daniel, she'd only known him a few months. Less than a year. He'd known and loved his father for his entire life.

"I'm so sorry, Brett." She didn't really know what

else to say. When someone is grieving a loss like that, there really is nothing to say. She knew that people's words had meant little to her these last few months.

"Thanks. It's been over three years now, but it's still hard."

"And your mother?"

"She passed away when I was a baby. My father raised me, made me who I am today." His voice caught in this throat for a moment. "Anyway, eventually, Ali was diagnosed with cancer. He died last year, but Amira took over. And, well… Amira has always been a bit…"

"Snotty? Witchy?"

Brett let out a big laugh. "Well, yes, but that's not what I was going to say."

"Sorry."

"She's kind of obsessed with… me."

"Oh," Paige said.

"She doesn't live on the property, but she does occasionally stay here when she doesn't want to drive back to Atlanta. She's here at least once every couple of weeks, mainly checking on her horses and preparing for shows. I don't get involved too much, but it does bring a small slice of income to the ranch, so it gives her yet another reason to spend time with me. And since I've been gone to Colorado for awhile, she's probably been antsy to start pursuing me again."

"Have you ever considered giving her a chance at winning your cowboy heart?" she asked with a smile.

"I don't think my cowboy heart could take that," he responded with a chuckle.

"Why are you telling me all of this?" Paige finally asked.

"I don't really know. You feel like... a friend?"

Her heart rate shot up and then back down. Why did the thought of being his friend make her happy and sad at the same time?

"So you want advice?" she asked with a smile.

"If you have some."

"I actually don't. She seems like a handful. I would just say to watch your back, Brett. That woman is bad news."

He sighed and nodded. "I'm afraid you might be right."

BRETT HAD THOROUGHLY ENJOYED his time sitting with Paige by the lake. But the incident with Amira showing up when she was supposed to be away for the weekend was frustrating. She was a poison in his life that he just couldn't seem to get rid of, and the last thing he wanted was for Paige to feel uncomfortable at Clover Lake.

After parting ways with Paige, Brett had gone to check on Aunt Elda who was snoozing in front of the TV. He woke her up and fed her some lunch - her favorite "farm" meal of black-eyed peas, raw onion and cornbread - and let her doze off again.

The truth was, his aunt was sleeping more and more, and that was starting to concern him. He planned to call the doctor to come see her at the ranch sometime before she left.

He also called The Cove and checked on the new temp girl who was running it for the next couple of days. She'd worked there as a temp the Christmas before, so she knew the ins and outs and seemed to have everything under control.

Paige had gone upstairs to change out of her "smelly horse clothes", as she put it. When she walked back downstairs, she was wearing a pair of jeans and a baby blue t-shirt that fit her in all the right spots. He looked down and noticed her wearing the same sneakers he saw before.

"Don't you own a pair of boots?" he asked with a laugh.

"I lived in New York City, Brett. Not much call

for cowboy boots there unless I wanted prissy socialites pointing and laughing at me."

"Well, then, maybe we need to run an errand."

"I don't need boots. I live by the beach now."

"Are you saying you'll never visit Clover Lake again after this weekend?"

She studied him carefully for a moment. "I think I would cry if I never got to visit here again."

He grinned. "Then lets get you a pair of boots that you can keep here when you need to get away."

"Get away from what?" she asked.

"Your own mind. Come on. We'll grab some lunch too."

A few minutes later, they were in the truck heading toward Savannah. Brett was excited to show her the sights, and she seemed excited too as she talked the whole way and pointed out things on the short drive into town.

"Gosh, I love this city. It's so historical and quaint," she said.

"Yeah. It feels like being transported back in time, doesn't it?"

Brett pulled up to a restaurant in the historic district. "You like seafood?"

"I love it, and I haven't had any good catfish in years."

He smiled. "Then you're going to love their pecan crusted catfish and homemade hushpuppies," he said.

He got out and she waited this time for him to open the door, which he considered progress. He opened it and helped her down, and then they walked toward the old, historic building. It was dark red brick with lush green plants lining the sidewalk near the door.

"The owner of this place was Jack Mallard, a good friend of my Dad's. His son, Mike, runs it now. Best seafood in the state, as far as I'm concerned."

They walked inside and got seated. Now he got to look at her. How would he stop himself from looking like some kind of weirdo?

She was just so different from any woman he'd ever met. Her hair was thick and wavy and dark, like sunshine mixed with milk chocolate. Her skin was what he would call fair, or maybe porcelain, with a smattering of light orange freckles dotting the bridge of her nose. But it was her lips he couldn't stop staring at. They were the perfect shade of pink without any lipstick and her top lip was upturned toward her nose as if it was begging to be bitten. By him.

He tried to think of manure again. It didn't work.

So he thought of Phil wearing lingerie and that did the trick for the time being.

"What can I get y'all to drink?" the waitress asked.

"I'll take sweet tea, light ice and no lemon, please," Paige said.

"I'll have the same," Brett said. The waitress laid two menus down and walked to the back. "Light ice and no lemon."

"What?"

"I've ordered the same thing for years. Just never heard anyone do the same."

She smiled. "Ice waters it down. Tea should be deep and dark and syrupy. And lemon, well... yuck."

Brett laughed. "I guess we have that in common, at least."

"I bet we have a lot of things in common, actually."

"Oh yeah? Let's test that. Favorite color?"

"Blue. And you?" she asked.

"Green."

"Darn. Okay, favorite dessert?"

"Peach cobbler."

"Love it, but my fave would have to be pound-cake. And I mean the good stuff made with butter-milk and the whole nine yards," she said.

"How did you ever survive as a Southerner in New York City?" He raised an eyebrow.

"I have no clue," she said smiling. "But now that I'm here, it feels like home. Weird because I have't ever been this far South."

"Well, I'm glad it feels like home."

The waitress brought their drinks, and they both took a sip before laughing at the same time.

"Perfection," she said, before closing her eyes and taking a long sip through her straw. His body was starting to react again, yet he couldn't stop watching her drink from the straw.

Brett was forced to think about Phil in lingerie again. Didn't work. That made him feel bad for a variety of reasons that only a psychotherapist could probably uncover.

"So, you were born in Tennessee but you ended up in New York. Care to tell that story?" Maybe talking would calm him back down.

Her face went blank and her eyes were staring right through him now. Mistake. He'd made a mistake.

"Sorry. Too personal..." he started.

"No. It's okay. I'm just not used to talking about myself all that much. But we're friends, and you told me about your Dad..."

"Still, you don't have to."

She thought for a moment and then smiled. "No. I want to." She took another sip of her drink and then drew in a deep breath. "I was born to a teenage mother with a love for alcohol and drugs and not so much a love for babies. She abandoned me at a church. It was on the news back then, apparently. I was bounced from foster home to foster home for years. I'm one of those kids who 'slipped through the cracks' without ever finding a real family. Had some bad things happen during that time…" Again, her eyes stared through him for a moment. It looked like she was watching an upsetting movie that he couldn't see.

"You don't have to talk about this, Paige."

She continued on like he didn't say anything. "Anyway, when I was a teenager, I was a handful, so they put me with this old woman known for taking in problem kids. She was good to me, protected me from anything else bad happening. But I gave her a rough time. When I was seventeen, she died. I had just graduated high school, so I took off, figuring by the time someone caught me I'd be eighteen anyway. I don't think anyone ever really looked for me. Slipped through the cracks again, I guess."

"Have you made a decision yet?" the waitress

asked, interrupting Paige and irritating Brett. He'd been so mesmerized by her story that he hadn't noticed the woman standing there waiting to take their order. They both ordered and Paige continued.

"I took a lot of odd jobs, lived as a homeless person, but finally made my way to New York. Long story short, got into working in catering. Found my own place. Things were looking up, and then I met Daniel."

Daniel. The fiance.

"His family is one of the wealthiest in the whole New England area. But he was different. Good. Giving. Wanted to be more than a rich guy. We hit it off and he proposed a few months later."

"Sounds like you really loved him a lot."

"I did. I still do… But there were issues. Actually, one main issue - his mother. She's an evil woman, and she tried to pay me off to leave him. There was no way she wanted the likes of me marrying her son."

Brett's blood felt like it was literally boiling. How could anyone not like Paige? He had this protective instinct over her, but it didn't make any logical sense. He'd only just met her.

"Seriously? I thought that kind of thing only happened in movies. Did Daniel know?"

She swallowed hard. "No. He never got to find out."

"I'm so sorry, Paige."

"And then she refused to let me see him after the accident. I waited in the hospital for hours every single day, and she wouldn't let me in. I couldn't see him or touch him or say goodbye. And then one day, he was gone. No funeral or anything. So I left. I couldn't stay there anymore. Reminders were everywhere. She kicked me out of his apartment, so I stayed with a friend until I could create a plan."

"Why January Cove?"

"You'll laugh." She explained the story of pointing to a map and selling her engagement ring.

"You are one amazing woman, Paige Emerson."

Her eyes widened as she looked at him. "What?"

"You have to be one of the most resilient people I've ever met. I've had my share of problems in life, but nothing even close to what you've experienced. You're really very impressive."

She blushed a bit and smiled. "Thanks. But I'd rather have avoided the problems and impressed you with my singing skills or something."

Brett laughed. "Can you sing?"

"I can't, which made for a very short-lived job as a street performer. People paid me to stop singing."

They both started laughing, and Brett couldn't remember a time he'd laughed as hard, especially with a woman. Normally, he found himself walking on eggshells, trying not to say the wrong thing or trying not to start an argument. But with Paige, everything was easy.

The waitress brought their food a few minutes later, and they ate while chatting about random things. Gossip in January Cove. Elda's younger years and how she was as a great aunt. How Brett learned to run the ranch. Nothing too heavy. They had already covered heavy topics enough for one day.

When they finished up, Brett paid the bill. "Ready to go look for some kicky Southern girl boots?"

"Of course," she said as she stood up.

They walked the short distance to a leather shop called The Tannery. Brett loved to come here and buy belts and boots and anything else he could find. It wasn't cheap, but it was quality stuff and lasted forever.

"What about these?" he asked, picking up a pair of brown cowboy boots with turquoise threading throughout and matching gemstones.

Paige's eyes got wide as she took the boot from his hand. "Oh my gosh, these are amazing! Look at the detail..." She turned the boot over and noticed it was her size, so she kicked off one shoe and slipped it on.

Brett couldn't help but watch her as she smiled and turned in front of the mirror. That happy look on her face was priceless, especially now that he knew more about what she'd been through her whole life. He felt like a protector, and as long as he could keep her in January Cove or Savannah, he'd make sure she felt happiness as often as possible.

Oh, man, this was bad. How was he already falling for her? No matter how he tried, he couldn't seem to help it. Conjuring Phil wearing lingerie AND manure didn't even help.

"I love these!" she said, a squeal in her voice.

Brett smiled. "Then get them. They look awesome on you."

Paige grinned and then reached inside the boot for the tag. When she did, she sucked in a sharp breath and sounded like she was choking. "We should go." She placed the boot back on the shelf before slowly letting go of it.

"What? Why?" Brett asked. He pulled the tag out and noticed the boots were $400.

"Brett, can we go?" she asked, not looking at him.

"Paige, what's wrong? Is it the price?" he whispered. She shot him a glaring look and walked out the door. He followed her outside a moment later and touched her arm. When she turned around, she had tears in her eyes.

"I'm sorry. I'm just being stupid." She sat down on a nearby park bench and stared at the moss-covered trees lining the street.

"You're not being stupid, Paige. I should've warned you about the prices in there. But the boots are high quality and will last for years..."

"It's not that. I'm sure they're worth it. It's just that it suddenly hit me in there."

"What did?"

She paused and sighed. "You know, I've been struggling my whole life. Struggling to make money, to keep a roof over my head, to eat. And maybe a part of me was happy to be with Daniel because I knew money would never be an issue again. I told myself that I didn't love him for his money and power, but I think a small part of me did, and that just made me feel like dirt."

Brett instinctively reached his arm around Paige. She looked at him for a moment and then laid her head on his shoulder. It wasn't romantic; it was more of a friendship feeling. But he was okay with that.

"Paige, you're a good person. You didn't love

Daniel for the money. I think you loved him for a lot of reasons, but part of that was probably the security he gave you. That's okay. Security comes in many forms. Apparently, he made you feel safe."

She took in a breath and then looked up at him, her eyes soft but intense. "I feel safe right now." She laid her head back down and they sat there for what seemed like hours but didn't feel like enough time at all.

CHAPTER 8

" *D*ang it. I dropped my keys back there somewhere. Do you mind grabbing us a couple of coffees while I go look for them?" Brett asked. Paige looked at him inquisitively, but decided she wanted some coffee too.

"Sure. But I'm buying," she said, turning before he could argue. She glanced back, but he was already gone, and then made her way to a small coffee shop next to the restaurant.

A few minutes later, she had two coffees in hand - well, actually one coffee and one sugar-laden latte for herself - and stood by the truck. When Brett appeared, he was hiding something behind his back.

"What are you up to?" she asked with a smile. He had a terrible poker face.

"Don't get mad." He pulled a brown shopping bag from behind his legs with The Tannery written on the side in Wild West lettering.

"Brett," she warned.

"Let me explain…"

"Why did you buy the boots? I don't need you to feel sorry for me. I thought you understood…"

"Paige. Please. Listen."

"I'm listening," she said, putting the coffee on the hood and crossing her arms. When the cups started sliding, Brett dropped the bag and grabbed them both.

"You're my friend and my employee. I asked you to come help me at the ranch for a few days, and you should be paid for that time."

"I don't make four-hundred dollars a weekend at the store, plus you're already paying me, Brett. Try again."

"Okay, fine. You need boots on a farm. I don't want to be responsible for messing up your spiffy sneakers there."

She tried not to smile, but she couldn't help it. "You hate my sneakers."

"I never said that."

"You didn't have to. And again, I appreciate the

thought, but I can't take these." She lifted the bag and held it out to him.

"Sorry. I lost the receipt. And they're non-refundable. And if I go back in there, they threatened to shoot me. Do you really want to be responsible for that?" He plastered on a fake, toothless grin.

"Why are you doing this?" she asked softly. "I wasn't trying to make you feel bad for me. I'm not that person."

He put the coffees on the curb and walked closer to her. She could feel her heart pounding in her chest, like a prisoner trying to get out of a cage.

"I know what kind of person you are, Paige. You're the kind of person who will put herself in harm's way for an old woman, even if it means tasering a stranger. You're the kind of person who will stand up to a rich woman no matter how much money she offers because you love her son. You're the kind of person who will listen and truly help someone who is dealing with an Alzheimer's diagnosis in their family. You're the kind of person I want to aspire to be. You're also the kind of person who deserves for someone to do something nice for her, and I'd selfishly like to be that person."

She stared up at him for a moment and then

hugged the shopping bag close to her. "Thank you. This is a very nice thing you've done, Brett Larson."

He reached down and picked up the coffees. "Let's go home."

Home?

THE RIDE back to Clover Lake was quieter, an air of tension overpowering the atmosphere inside the truck. Paige didn't really know what to say, and he didn't seem to know either. So, she looked out the window for most of the trip, taking in the sights and enjoying the spring air that was blowing in her face.

"Can I show you something?" Brett asked as they pulled back up the driveway at the ranch.

"Sure."

They stopped about halfway down the drive and he helped her jump down from the truck. "Might need those boots now."

She smiled and pulled them from the bag as she sat on the running board of the vehicle. She slipped off her sneakers and tossed them in the floorboard before sliding the boots onto her feet.

Brett reached back and took her hand, leading her through some thick brush. A jolt of electricity shot through her hand and up her arm, and it was unlike anything she'd ever felt. But she didn't pull away because it felt good to have Brett holding her hand, and that thought alone scared the crap out of her.

They walked for a few minutes, and she was very glad to be wearing her new boots because the brush was pretty thick and snakes were known to be in places like this. As the woods thinned out, she heard running water and could see it sparkling in the afternoon sun between the trees. When they were finally out of the thicker woods, the sight in front of her was astounding.

It was a wide creek with crystal clear water and a small waterfall raining down on the side. There were thousands of smooth rocks and pebbles of every color imaginable under the water, and moss growing on most of the trees and larger jagged rocks nearby. The sunlight streamed in through the surrounding trees, making a beautiful artistic pattern of darks and lights.

Around them was deafening silence except for the sound of the waterfall, lazily cascading over the rocks, and the occasional bird chirping in a tall tree nearby.

"Wow. What is this place?" she asked, whispering

as if she would damage the beauty by talking too loudly.

Brett smiled broadly. "This is where Aunt Elda got married."

Inexplicably, the thought of that brought tears to Paige's eyes. She tried to imagine a young Elda standing by the creek making vows to the man she loved, a man she would be married to for almost fifty years. She was still holding Brett's hand for some reason, so she used her free hand to quickly brush the stray droplet away from her cheek before he could see it.

"It's stunning. Truly beautiful. I could stay here forever."

"Then let's sit down," he said, pulling her toward a large rock that overlooked the creek. He climbed up, letting go of her hand, and she felt the void. But then he reached down and took both of her hands, pulling her up onto the rock beside him. There was no space between their bodies now as they sat side by side staring into the shallow creek bed below.

For awhile, neither of them said anything, and that was okay. Paige assumed this was what she'd heard people refer to as "companionable silence".

"One day, I want to get married here too," Brett

said softly. Her heart squeezed so tight, she felt she might be having a heart attack.

"Oh yeah?" she managed to breathe out. "I didn't know guys thought about stuff like that."

Brett chuckled under his breath. "Most guys probably don't."

"What about cowboys?" she asked, bumping her shoulder into his.

"Cowboys probably don't either."

"You're a different kind of cowboy. They broke the mold with you, Brett Larson."

"Maybe so. And that's probably a good thing."

"I doubt it. You don't seem to have any faults."

He looked at her and shot her a dimpled smile. "Not true."

"Okay. Tell me some of your terrible faults."

"Well, I sometimes forget to put the toilet seat down."

She put her hand over her mouth in mock shock. "Oh, how terrible for a man who lives alone to not put the toilet seat down!"

"Very funny. You're pretty perfect yourself there, Miss Paige."

"Not even close. I'm stubborn and moody and short."

"No, you're a fighter, you don't take any crap from people and you're adorably petite."

Her mouth dropped open when he said it. Then he looked like a deer caught in the headlights. Brett cleared his throat.

"So, I brought you here to ask you what you think about building a small chapel right over there..." he said, obviously changing the subject since his voice went three levels higher in volume.

"For the wedding venue rental stuff? Yeah, that would be really cool..." Really cool? Dear God, she sounded like a stupid teenager right now.

"I don't want to put it too close. This creek floods a couple of times a year at least. It'd have to go over there in the flat space," he said, pointing off in the distance. But she wasn't looking where he was pointing. Nope, she was looking at the thin line of stubble already forming across his jawline. And she wanted to run her tongue across it.

What in the world was wrong with her?

"I can do most of the work myself, I think," he continued. "I still need to show you the barn. I think it'd be a great place for receptions and maybe even corporate events."

"There are lots of opportunities here, for sure."

Now she was just using filler words because all she could think about was his warm body sitting against hers and the feel of his hand in hers a few minutes ago.

Guilt settled into her stomach like an old enemy, bringing with it queasiness. Daniel was gone, but every time she felt like her life could start moving again, like falling in love was at least a possibility, the guilt took her by the throat and shoved her against the wall.

"Want to go see the barn now?" Brett asked.

She swallowed hard. "No. Actually, I think I'd like to go check on Elda and maybe take a nap myself. I'm a little tired."

He studied her carefully and then nodded, but she could tell he wasn't buying her story of being tired. Women in their twenties rarely took afternoon naps, and she definitely didn't.

"Sure, okay," he said. "Not a problem." He climbed off the rock and reached up to help her. Paige shook her head.

"I've got it," she said, forcing a smile. Only she didn't have it, especially not with brand new, unfamiliar boots on. Instead, she toppled off the rock and narrowly missed slamming her head into the ground. Brett caught her in mid-air but lost his footing on the wet embankment which sent them both into the water with Paige flat on her back.

"We've got to stop meeting like this," he said softly.

Time stood still, like in a movie. She couldn't hear anything but the soft sound of the babbling brook and the two of them breathing. His face was inches from hers, and his eyes were caring. His lips were... available.

Without thinking, she reached up and pulled his face to hers, his warm lips pressing against her own, as anxious and willing as hers were. His tongue slipped between her lips and found hers.

He slid his hands under her head, cradling it in front of him and holding her in place. The water was cool, but not freezing, and she could've stayed there all day in his arms. Against his chest. Attached to his lips.

There was a strong need to keep kissing him, to feel the presence of a man who wanted her. To feel passion again. To feel desired. To feel like a woman.

And then the guilt crawled up from her gut and wrenched its evil claws around her brain and snapped her out of the romantic moment.

No, the guilt said, *you're never meant to be happy*

again. You don't deserve it. Daniel was your one true love, and you're cheating on him right now.

She pulled away and bolted upright, almost head butting Brett in the process.

"Are you okay?" he asked, touching her on the shoulder.

"I'm sorry. I shouldn't have done that. I just got caught up in the moment..." She stood to her feet and climbed back onto dry ground before she collapsed onto the grass in a heap with her head resting on her knees.

Brett sat down beside her. "You don't have to feel guilty, Paige. It's okay to have feelings again."

How did he know what she was thinking? Maybe he was a psychic cowboy. But for some reason, she matched his kindness with anger.

"How do you know anything about what I feel, Brett? Have you ever even been in love? Have you ever lost the love of your life?"

He sighed. "You're right. I have no idea what either of those things feel like, Paige. But I know that if Daniel was in love with you, he'd want you to be happy."

She stood and started pacing back and forth. "Oh, and I suppose you think that means I should be with you?"

"I didn't say that…"

"We just met! And you're my boss!"

Brett stood and stopped her from pacing. "Paige, calm down. It was just a kiss. We were in the moment. No big deal. Okay?"

No big deal? Had she mis-read him? Maybe to him she was an easy mark, a possible one-night stand. That thought made her angry and sad and disappointed at the same time. Now she really did need a nap because it was the only way to escape from feeling everything.

"Take me back to the house. Please."

"Paige…"

"I don't want to talk about this anymore. I don't." She stared at him - actually, she glared at him - and he obliged.

Not another word was spoken during the drive or when she jumped out of the truck, wet and mentally drained - and ran into the house.

THERE WAS a lot Brett would never understand about women. Their moods. Their secrets. Their needs.

Actually, there was a lot he'd never understand about Paige Emerson.

Maybe she was right. They barely knew each other, and he was her boss. Had he taken advantage of her at the creek? After all, she had kissed him first, a fact that shocked and aroused him at the same time.

When she'd reached up and pulled his lips to hers, he had never been more thankful for anything in his life. And kissing her had been like going to heaven. He'd never kissed a woman like her before. There was so much raw emotion, so much need behind her kiss. Like she'd been walking through a desert for days without water, and he was a big juicy glass of it.

But what did he know about her loss? He couldn't feel what she felt. He couldn't understand what it meant to love someone enough to agree to marry them and then have them die so suddenly. He'd been in love before, at least thought it was love at the time. Still, he'd never really thought he was looking at the woman he'd still be loving when he was an old man.

Until today.

No. Stop thinking that way. It was just a kiss, you said so yourself. Just a kiss. Nothing more. No big deal.

Only, that was a lie. Now he was having a hard

time picturing himself ever kissing another woman like that again.

He ran the brush across Noelle and kissed her on the cheek. "Maybe you're the only girl for me," he said with a sad chuckle.

"You're going to have a heck of a time finding a wedding dress to fit her."

Brett turned to see Paige standing there, her eyes red and puffy from obvious crying. He wanted to reach out and pull her into a hug, but recent history told him not to make that move.

"Hey," he said, simply. That had to be safe.

"Hey. Listen, I wanted to come say that I'm so sorry for how I acted earlier. I'm just dealing with a lot of stuff…"

"I won't say I understand the stuff you're dealing with. But I understand your reaction. No need to apologize."

"No, I do need to apologize." She leaned against the door to the stall and ran her hand across Noelle. "I started it, and then I basically blamed you."

"Well… Yeah, I can't argue with that." Paige laughed which allowed Brett to relax a little. "I like you, Paige. A lot."

She sucked in a deep breath. "Jeez, you're one honest cowboy."

"Guilty as charged," he said as he set the brush on a table and leaned against the wall of the stable.

"This feels too fast, Brett."

Brett closed the distance between them. "Do you like me, Paige?"

"Of course. We said we were friends…"

"You know what I'm asking."

She swallowed and held his gaze. "I'm having some feelings, yes. But I'm not sure I can act on those feelings… again."

"Look," he said softly. "I'm just as blown away by this as you are. I've never felt this way, and certainly not about a woman who tased me the moment we met."

Paige giggled. "How many times do I have to apologize?"

He took a chance and reached out to hold both of her hands. To his surprise, she let him.

"I'm not asking for forever, Paige. I don't even know what I want. I just know that I like being with you more than anyone else, and when I'm not around you I feel a void. So maybe we can just take things slow? Maybe go on a date or two?"

She looked down at her feet and bit her lips together. Finally, she looked up. "I can't promise anything, but I'd like to spend more time hanging out with you."

He sighed in relief and smiled. "That sounds perfect."

BRETT AND PAIGE made a pact to keep their possible budding romance private, especially when it came to Elda. They didn't want to get her hopes up or make things uncomfortable when they were all together.

"Pass the potatoes, please," Elda said as they sat at dinner that night. Paige had to admit that having a big home cooked meal at Clover Lake was like being home again, only she'd never really had a home. It certainly had no resemblance to her life in a penthouse apartment; those were two very different situations.

But she found herself smiling more and enjoying the peace of being away from it all. She'd miss Clover Lake when they went back to January Cove tomorrow, but she loved it there too.

"Here you go, Miss Elda," she said as she scooped potatoes onto Elda's plate. Brett smiled at her across the table, and butterflies attacked her stomach.

Part of the guilt she felt wasn't because of Daniel

really. It was because of what she was feeling. She'd loved Daniel more than she thought was possible after coming from a life of no one really loving her. His love was a miracle to her, something she'd never seen coming or even expected. It was like being given a piece of bread after not eating for a month.

But what Brett was making her feel was different. Maybe better. And that alone was guilt-inducing. Just the way Brett was - opening doors, catching her when she fell, making her laugh - made her heart skip a beat.

Her feelings were making her feel guilty, as if caring for Brett made her love of Daniel something that wasn't real. And questioning her love of Daniel was something she wasn't ready to do and probably never would be.

"I saw where you got married today, Miss Elda. It's a beautiful spot."

Elda looked up and smiled. "A lot of love in that place. A lot of love." Paige tried not to look at Brett, but she couldn't help it.

"It was the start of a fairytale romance," Paige said, referring to Elda's marriage.

"And more to come," she replied before taking another bite of her food.

"Enjoying your food?" Brett asked. He'd grilled

steaks for them and made mashed potatoes. Elda had made a pound cake that they'd be enjoying after dinner, if she could stay awake.

"It's wonderful."

"Probably not as good as those fancy New York City restaurants you've been to," Brett said with a smile.

"Better."

CHAPTER 9

"*S*o? How's the trip going?" Sandi asked from the other end of the line.

"It's not really considered a trip when you're less than forty-five minutes from home," Paige said with a laugh. "And it's going good. Really good."

"Oooohhh... That sounds promising. What does 'really good' mean? Like naked cowboy good?"

"You have a one track mind!"

"Yeah, but it's a pretty interesting track, right?"

Paige sighed and fell back onto her bed. "I kissed him."

"What? Oh my God! Seriously? What did he do? Did you like it? Are you guys dating?"

"Calm down, Sandi! Jeez. You need to stop drinking so much coffee!"

"This is so exciting! When can I meet him?"

"First of all, it was an accident."

"An accident? As in your lips got lost or went crazy and attached themselves to his?"

"Sort of. I don't know. We were laying in the water at the creek and…"

"That sounds hot…"

"Shut up. We fell off an embankment and into the creek. I was on the bottom and for reasons I still can't explain or comprehend, I reached up and kissed him."

"Wow. That's not like you at all, Paige."

"I know!"

"Maybe you just need some, you know, male attention…"

"No, it's more than that. And that's what's scaring me."

PAIGE WALKED DOWNSTAIRS on her last morning at Clover Lake and sighed as she stared out the floor to ceiling windows that had been added to the back of the house. They definitely weren't original to the place, but they offered a spectacular view of the pastures and the amazing orange-tinted sunrise.

"Good morning," she heard Elda say from a chair by the fireplace.

"Oh, Miss Elda, you scared me," Paige said with her hand to her chest. The old woman was so small and frail that she didn't see her sitting there.

"Sorry, dear," she said with a sweet smile. "I just love to watch the sunrise here."

Paige sat down on the sofa and looked out the window, taking in the serenity of the morning. "I do too. The sunrises here are different than in the city. No distractions from the beauty, I guess."

"Oh, country sunrises are the best. Have you enjoyed your time at Clover Lake, my dear?"

Paige smiled. "Yes. I've never felt so immediately at home anywhere in my life."

"Maybe God had you travel to a lot of places so that, in this moment, you'd appreciate what home feels like."

Paige took her words in for a moment. "Maybe so."

"If there's one thing I've learned in all my years on this Earth, it's that nothing that happens to us is accidental."

"You don't think so?"

"I know it, deep in my soul. Each situation that

we find ourselves in is a lesson and a blessing, whether we see it at the time or not."

"It's hard to believe that when I've had so much loss in my life, I suppose." Paige wished she could share in Elda's certainties about life. Maybe when she was in her 90s, she would.

"Loss is inevitable, sweetie. It's gonna happen whether we like it or not. But it's what we do after a loss that makes us either a victor or a victim. I see you as a victor, Paige." She reached over and took Paige's hand.

"You do? I sure don't feel like one some days."

"A woman never feels like she's strong enough for all that life throws at her, but we are. We're stronger than we will ever know, Paige. You've risen above a life full of struggle, a life that many people would've given up on. And here you are, with me, watching the beauty of a sunrise. You've made it through."

Paige felt her eyes welling with tears, so she sat back and faced the sunrise again, still holding Elda's hand.

"Thank you, Elda."

PAIGE STOOD in her bedroom and looked around. She was going to miss Clover Lake, but she was pretty sure she'd be back soon. Brett had run into town to gas up his truck while she packed her things.

She heard a knock at the door and swung it open, assuming it was Brett telling her he was ready to go. Instead, she was shocked to find Amira standing there in all her supermodel glory.

She was wearing a very low-cut red top with tight jeans and cowboy boots. Paige suddenly felt short, stumpy and in need of a paper bag to put over her head.

"Good morning, Paige. That is your name, right?" she said, a hint of an accent making her even more perfect.

"Yes. How can I help you?"

"May I come in?"

Paige nodded and stepped back. She stood next to the bed, not sitting down because she didn't want to invite Amira to stay long. But Amira sat down on the chair in front of the vanity anyway. She looked at herself in the mirror for a moment before turning back to Paige.

"Listen, Paige," she said, holding her name out in some kind of insulting way, "I know that you have some feelings for Brett."

"Excuse me?"

"I saw you at the creek the other day."

"Were you following us? Brett said you didn't live here."

"I own part of this property, Paige. I can go where I like."

"You need to leave," Paige said, walking to the door and opening it. When Amira didn't budge, she closed the door and crossed her arms.

"Brett is my boyfriend, Paige."

Paige could feel her heart beating wildly as it crawled up her throat and threatened to shoot out of her mouth. "What?"

"He won't tell you because I'm sure he doesn't want to hurt you, but we've been together off and on for years now. Since we were kids. And that isn't likely to change. I'd hate to see you get hurt."

Paige couldn't speak. She was torn between believing that Brett had lied to her and trusting a guy she hardly knew.

"I understand you've already lost one man recently…"

"Shut your mouth," Paige said, taking a step forward. "You don't know anything about me."

"Oh, but I do. You see, I have ties to New York

City. I know all about Daniel and how his mother hated you so much…"

"I'm warning you," Paige said, wondering mentally if she'd get in trouble for using the stun gun in this particular situation.

"Keep your hands off Brett. Do you understand me?" Amira said, rising up and facing Paige.

"Or what?" Paige asked, even though she had no plans to start something with a man who was already taken.

"You don't want to know, trust me. Brett is going to marry me, Paige. No one is going to stand in the way of that." She stared at Paige with her ice cold blue eyes for a moment and then slowly strolled out of the room, leaving Paige to sort out the mess that was her life yet again.

PAIGE DRAGGED her bag down the stairs and set it by the front door. She couldn't wait to get home and out of this mess with Brett. Thoughts of quitting The Cove flashed through her mind, and it made her sad. She liked her job.

"Your carriage awaits, madam," Brett said with a

big smile as he bowed when he opened the front door. "Ready to go?"

"Yes," Paige said without looking at him. She picked up her bag, but he tried to take it from her hand. She pulled back. "I've got it."

Brett stood there looking at her from the porch as she walked down to the truck and tossed her bag in the back. Elda was already sitting inside, her eyes closed. Paige opened her door before Brett could get back to the truck and climbed inside, carefully shutting it so as not to wake Elda.

He locked up the house and climbed into the truck before looking at Paige. "You okay?"

"Fine. Can we go?" She turned and looked out her window, praying he would crank the car soon. After a few moments, he did and they were on their way.

BRETT WAS THINKING about becoming a monk. A monastery would be woman-free, right?

These were the types of thoughts he had when he didn't understand women. As far as he knew, Paige was not mad at him a few hours before, but now she wasn't speaking or even looking his direction, and he had no idea what had caused the shift.

He pulled up to Elda's house and helped her inside and then returned to the truck. He was half surprised that Paige hadn't bolted from the vehicle while he was gone for those few minutes, but there she was, staring at absolutely nothing out her window when he came back.

He could've easily taken Paige home first since he was staying at Elda's, but he wanted some time alone with her to try to figure out what had happened. If she didn't speak to him, that wouldn't be possible.

"So," he said as he backed out of the driveway, "would you be interested in having dinner with me tonight?"

"No. Thank you." She didn't look his way, opting instead to stare down at her phone which wasn't even on.

"Okay... How about tomorrow night? There's a great steakhouse off Baker Avenue..."

"No."

"Paige, I'm sensing a shift here. Are you mad at me for something?" he asked as he turned onto the main road. He could hear her breathing deeply, and he was pretty sure some kind of rage was boiling just below the surface.

"I'm not mad at you, Brett. You're my boss, and that's all we can be."

"What? I don't understand..." he said as he pulled into her driveway. Paige opened her door almost before he could stop the truck and got out. She tried to reach into the back to get her bag, but she was far too short to do it.

Brett got out and walked around. He stood in front of her and crossed his arms.

"Give me my bag. Please."

"No."

"Excuse me?"

"No. I'm not giving you your bag until you tell me what's going on. One minute we're kissing, then you're mad, then you apologize and agree to try getting to know each other better... and now you're acting like I killed your puppy or something."

He could've sworn she almost smiled, but then the look of anger planted itself on her face and set up camp. He didn't like that look on her. He missed her smile already, and confusion clouded his thoughts.

"I don't date liars," she said before she stepped up onto the running board she'd apparently just noticed, grabbed her bag and turned toward her house.

"Liar? What did I lie about?" he asked, following her to the door. She keyed the lock quickly and opened it.

"Ask Amira," she said as she slammed the door shut in his face. Oh, he definitely planned to ask Amira.

PAIGE LEANED back against the arm of the sofa and stretched her back against it. She'd been sitting there for hours now, trying to read a book but re-reading the same line over and over again.

She couldn't stop thinking about Brett and the way he'd looked at her when she accused him of lying. Had she been wrong about him? He looked shell-shocked, especially when she said Amira's name.

Probably because he got busted.

It was close to midnight, and she knew she should get to bed. Work was going to come early the next morning, and she could only hope that Brett didn't show up at the bookstore.

As she was turning off the lights in the living room, she heard noises outside. She grabbed her taser and crept toward the front door, ready to shock anyone who tried to get in. The sounds stopped, but a few moments later someone knocked - actually banged - on her door. She could hear what sounded like a struggle and a woman's voice too.

Worried about the woman, she cracked the door open, but the person pushed into it enough for the door to open all the way. She couldn't see who it was or how many of them there were, so she reached out with her stun gun and pressed the button.

"Ouch! Stop it! Oh my God, you lunatic!" the woman screamed. Oh, crap, she got the woman who was being attacked instead of the man.

She flipped on the foyer light in an effort to see the pair so she could get a better shot at the man, but it was Brett. And Amira.

"What in the hell?" Paige said, dropping the taser on the table and stepping back from them both. She could hardly catch her breath she was so scared.

"This is how you say hello? You electrocute me?" Amira screeched. She was holding her upper arm, and seeing the look of pain on her face actually made Paige want to smile.

"Brett, do you want to explain what's going on here? I heard voices outside. You're lucky I didn't shoot you both!"

"You have a gun too?" Amira asked, still rubbing her arm and furrowing her eyebrows at Paige.

"No comment."

"Can we come in? I'd hate for the neighbors to call the cops," Brett said. Paige nodded and walked back to the living room.

"It's almost midnight. Why are you here?" She sat down on the sofa and crossed her arms.

"Go ahead, Amira. Tell her," Brett said in a firm voice. Amira jutted out her chin and blinked her eyes slowly. "Now."

"Fine!" she said, blowing out a sharp breath. "We're not lovers."

Paige felt butterflies in her stomach once again. "What?"

"And?" Brett said to Amira.

"And we never were." She said it so softly that Paige could barely hear her.

"I don't understand. Why would you tell me that?"

"Because he should be with me." Amira wasn't looking at her or Brett. "I mean, look at me." Nothing was wrong with her self-confidence, that was for sure.

"That was a cruel, selfish thing to do. And the things you said about Daniel and me…"

"Wait. She talked about Daniel?" Brett asked, anger apparent on his face.

"I just mentioned him. Relax," Amira said, rolling her eyes.

"You need to go," Brett said. "You've done enough damage here. I texted for a cab on the way here. They should be outside waiting to take you home. And notice I said home, not Clover Lake. Our business is done. Don't come back there or I'll have you arrested. Do you understand me?"

This side of Brett was new. The fighter. The defender. The no-nonsense ass kicking cowboy. Paige liked it a little more than she cared to admit.

Amira skulked out of the house like a wet cat and slammed the door behind her. Brett watched her go, peeked out the window to see if she got in the cab and then turned to Paige.

"I'm so incredibly sorry for what she said. None of it was true. I told you she was obsessed, and I guess I should've remedied this problem years ago." He sat down on the coffee table across from Paige.

"I should've asked you, Brett. I didn't handle that very well."

He smiled. "I bought her out tonight."

Paige's eyes went wide. "I can't believe she agreed."

"I made it very clear to her that I would have nothing else to do with her and that she'd have to deal with Lou on all financial matters, and she hates Lou. I said she'd have no access to me at all, and she caved. My attorney brought over the paperwork, I scratched out a painful check and we were done."

"I'm happy for you. That will certainly make things easier on you." She rubbed her hands together anxiously, unsure of where this was going.

"Paige, will you please go to dinner with me tomorrow night?" he asked softly.

"You still want to see me? Even after all of this?"

"This wasn't your fault."

"I didn't trust you."

"You don't really know me well enough to trust me like that. I don't blame you."

Paige stood up and walked across the room to her bookshelf, lifting a first-edition copy of Gone With The Wind from her line of books. She brought it to her chest and hugged it close.

"You know, Daniel bought this for me. He knew my favorite book of all time is Gone With The Wind. This is a first-edition copy of it."

Brett remained seated on the table and said nothing.

"I remember being so excited when he gave it to

me," she said softly, still not turning around. "I had never had anyone actually ask me about any of my favorite things. Not my favorite color or my favorite song. No one ever seemed to care much about what I wanted or needed."

She walked back to the sofa, still holding the book, and sat down. She opened it and ran her fingers across several of the pages.

"He had it wrapped in this beautiful gold foil paper with a bright red bow. I had never opened such a gorgeous gift before; I had only seen them at weddings I was helping at or on TV. But this was just for me, and it was all about me. I remember being so overwhelmed that I cried like a baby, and poor Daniel didn't know what was wrong with me."

She didn't know why she was suddenly spewing all of this information out at Brett, a guy she hardly knew. But for some reason it seemed necessary to get it all out, to have Brett know something about Daniel.

"It wasn't about what he spent or how it was wrapped. It was about someone finally caring enough to ask me what my favorite book was, and then caring enough to find a rare copy, and even caring enough to have it wrapped like it was being given to a queen or something." She finally looked up and smiled. Brett smiled back and reached out to hold the book. She slowly handed it to him and he looked down to study it for a moment before handing it back.

"Daniel sounds like a very nice guy, and I'm so glad he treated you well, Paige. You deserve that."

She bit both of her lips and then placed the book on the side table. "Daniel will always be a part of me, Brett, and I don't know if you're ready to have him included in a relationship. It's so soon, but I also have feelings... for you... and that makes me feel awfully guilty."

"Paige, we can go as slow as you need to go. And I will welcome Daniel because he helped make you into the woman sitting here across from me right now. I would never expect you to give up your memories of him."

She stared at him for a moment, fighting back the tears that were threatening to spill out at any moment, and reached for his hands.

"Then yes, I will go to dinner with you tomorrow night, Brett Larson."

CHAPTER 10

*P*aige hadn't slept much at all last night. After Brett left, she tried everything from meditation to a hot bath to melatonin, but nothing was sending her off to dream land.

So she did the only logical thing - she found her way to Jolt before work and downed a double espresso.

"Wow, you're here bright and early this morning," Rebecca said as she took Paige's order. "And you look exhausted. Are you okay, honey?"

"I am exhausted," Paige said, the bags under her eyes apparent. "Need a serious pick-me-up."

Rebecca took the order and Paige found a seat in the empty coffee shop. Even for the regulars, it was still very early.

Paige stared out across the street, over the ocean. Living in January Cove was like living on vacation, and sometimes she found it hard to believe that she had the good fortune to find a place like this to call home.

"Okay, so you want to tell me what's going on?" Rebecca asked with a smile as she set the coffee on the table. She slid into the chair across from Paige.

Paige knew that it was time to tell Rebecca her story. The whole story. So she started spilling it out, bit by bit, from being abandoned as a baby to losing Daniel to the new situation with Brett.

To her surprise, Rebecca just listened, nodding along and occasionally making a noise to let Paige know she was listening.

"I met him the other day," Rebecca said.

"Brett?"

"Yep. He came in for a latte. Nice guy. Loves his aunt."

"He's a wonderful guy…" Paige said softly.

"So what's the problem?"

"Guilt."

"Can I ask you something?"

"Sure," Paige said, taking a sip of her coffee.

"If Daniel appeared here right now, would you be

able to walk away from January Cove without any feelings for Brett?"

Paige thought for a moment. No one had ever quite put it to her that way. A few weeks ago, she would've left January Cove behind in a heartbeat if her beloved Daniel had shown up at her door. But now, after making a life for herself and meeting Brett, it wouldn't be so easy.

"No. I wouldn't," Paige said softly. Rebecca nodded and smiled.

"Then I think you have your answer. Give Brett a chance. Be vulnerable and cut yourself some slack when you have those moments of grief. If Brett is worthy of you, he'll understand and welcome memories of Daniel into your relationship."

"Is that what Jackson did?"

Rebecca smiled broadly, her eyes full of dreaminess at the mention of Jackson's name. From what little she had told Paige, Jackson Parker was a godsend after raising her son alone for so many years.

"That and more. Jackson accepted me for who I was and where I was in my life at the time. He accepted my son, Leo. And he accepted my late husband too because he will always be a part of our family."

"Thanks, Rebecca. I really appreciate you listening to me this morning. It helps more than you know. I'd better get to work."

Paige stood up and took a final gulp of her coffee before grabbing her purse.

"Good luck!" Rebecca called as she waved at Paige.

She was going to need it.

PAIGE ARRIVED at the bookstore full of renewed enthusiasm. She hoped to see Brett today, although for all she knew he was at the ranch for the day.

She was excited for their dinner date tonight, although she had no idea what to wear or where they were going. The excitement was something she hadn't experienced since her first date with Daniel many months ago.

As she started to straighten up the bookshelves, the store phone rang.

"Thanks for calling The Cove. This is Paige. How can I..."

"Paige! Thank God I found you. I need your help."

"Brett? Is everything okay?" He sounded

completely frantic and overwrought which was not at all like his regular personality.

"No. No, I'm not okay. Can you come to Elda's house? Just close the store and come, okay?" He hung up before she could ask questions. Paige turned off the lights, flipped the closed sign and locked the door before taking off toward Elda's house on foot.

By the time she reached Elda's front door, she was out of breath. She leaned over to catch her breath and then knocked on the door, but it was cracked open.

"Brett?" she called from the entryway. He came from around the corner, his face pale and drained of energy.

"Paige," he whispered, walking to her and holding onto her for dear life. He held her there as if his life depended on it. She pulled him closer and stood there, determined to be quiet and let him have whatever he needed in that moment. In reality, she already knew what this was about.

Elda was gone.

When he finally let her go, he looked down at her with tears in his eyes. "I'm supposed to be strong."

"You're supposed to be human," she said,

reaching up and putting her hand on his cheek. "She's gone?"

He nodded quickly and then sank down into a chair nearby. Paige started to sit on the arm of the chair, but he pulled her onto his knee and held her waist.

"I know she was old, but she's meant so much to me in my life. Treated me like a grandson instead of a great nephew. Hell, she's been my best friend many times in my life."

Paige pulled his head against her shoulder and pressed her lips into his hair. "It doesn't matter how old she was, Brett. You loved her and you always will."

"Did someone call for help?" a paramedic said, poking his head through the open front door.

Paige and Brett stood. "Yes. My great aunt... she passed in her sleep."

"Down the hall," Paige said, pointing beside them. The two EMTs rolled a stretcher into the house and toward Elda's room. Brett turned the other direction and walked outside, taking a deep breath.

Paige walked up behind him and slid her arms around his waist. It felt so natural to comfort him, to be his rock during a trying time. In fact, she felt like she'd known him forever in this moment.

"Thanks for coming when I called," he said softly.

She let go and walked in front of him. "Of course I came. Why wouldn't I?"

"You don't know me all that well yet, and we've had a bumpy road these last couple of days. Just... thank you."

"Brett, I loved Elda too."

He nodded and pulled her closer, and the two of them stood there for what seemed like hours while the medics rolled Elda out of the house and into the ambulance.

THE MEMORIAL SERVICE for Elda was small, as expected, given that most of her family had passed away before her. There were some distant cousins, a few old friends and many January Cove residents who knew her from the bookstore. Her passing was so sudden that a lot of people who lived out of town weren't able to make it.

Rebecca and Jackson came, along with Addison and Clay, most of them having known her their whole lives.

"Do you think she would've liked the service?" Brett asked as they left the tiny, country church on the outskirts of January Cove. It was white with a real steeple and stained glass windows.

"I do. It was no-frills, and we both know Miss Elda was a no-frills kind of woman," Paige said with a laugh.

"True. Since Elda wished to be cremated, I would like to spread her ashes on our family property. I thought it might be nice to spend another weekend there, just remembering her and honoring the legacy she left."

"That sounds like a great idea, Brett. And I can handle the store alone, no problem…"

"No. Paige, I meant that I wanted you to come."

Paige's heart started to pound. Spend the weekend on the ranch with Brett alone? The thought both excited and terrified her at the same time.

"Okay," she heard herself saying without thinking.

"Okay? I'm so glad you said yes," Brett said. "And we can finally have our date too."

"What?"

"Our dinner date. I didn't forget," he said. She smiled for the first time in days. Her date with Brett had been something to look forward to after months of feeling like there would never be any light at the end of the tunnel.

"I can't wait," she said, struggling not to blush for some reason.

PAIGE WALKED SLOWLY down the sidewalks of January Cove, taking in the smell of the salty air and the quaint shops on Main Street. She loved this place like she had lived here all of her life.

Everyone was nice and friendly. They waved when she walked by. It was as if her past didn't matter to anyone here since they all had stories of their own.

"Hey, Paige!" Addison Parker called from the garden in front of her B&B as she walked by. Addy's Inn was the place she had stay temporarily when she first arrived in January Cove a few months ago. It had felt like a real home to her, complete with home-cooked meals and rocking chair talks on the front porch.

"Hey, Addy," she said.

"How's Brett doing? I know he was so close to Miss Elda." She put down her pruning shears and walked to the other side of the white picket fence that ran across the front of her property.

"I think he's doing well. We're going out to

Clover Lake this weekend to spread her ashes where he grew up."

"Oh, what a nice thing for him to do. That's exactly where she should be. Listen, would you like to come in for some coffee?"

"Thanks for the invitation, but I've got to run by the bookstore to give the temp some instructions before Brett picks me up a little later."

Addy smiled. "I understand. Maybe when you get back? I miss having our talks on the porch," she said with a smile.

"I do too. Let's definitely get together when I get back." She waved and started walking toward the bookstore.

"Because I'm sure you'll have plenty to talk about when you get back!" Addy called to her with a giggle. Paige rolled her eyes and just kept walking.

As THEY PULLED BACK down the long dirt road to Clover Lake, Paige started to relax immediately. There was just something about this place that calmed her soul at the deepest levels.

Maybe it was the smell of grass clippings and the crispness of the warm spring air. The sky seemed bluer here, and the sound of birds chirping in the trees took every ounce of her stress away.

Clover Lake - and January Cove - were both so far removed from anywhere she'd lived in her life. New York City had been beautiful in its own way, of course, but there was never quiet there. Never the sound of a bird chirping nearby, and she hadn't realized until now how much she had missed that sound.

Of course, there had been plenty of pigeons, but most New Yorkers thought they were basically flying rats and not worthy of the title "bird". She tended to agree with that thought process.

Brett stopped the truck in front of the house and got out. He opened her door, helped her to the ground and grabbed both of their bags from the back.

"Ready?" he said, his voice a little lower and gruffer than normal, sending chills up and down her spine.

"Yes," she said with a smile.

This trip was about Elda and laying her to rest in the place where she spent most of her life. No matter how attracted she was to Brett, this wasn't the weekend to act on that. Unless he wanted to, of course. She mentally threw a bucket of cold ice water on her face.

"I thought we'd just relax tonight, eat some dinner. Then we can have a proper remembrance of Aunt Elda tomorrow. That okay with you?" he asked as they stopped in the foyer.

"Of course. Whatever you want, Brett."

He smiled. "Good. I'm going to go chat with Lou and Phil, let them know we're here. I'll let you get settled in."

IF HE WAS REALLY honest with himself, this trip was just as much about spending more time alone with Paige as it was about Elda. He surely wanted to be honorable about spreading her ashes, but somewhere from the great beyond he could hear his aunt cheering him on about falling for Paige.

Yep. He was falling for Paige.

There was no doubt about it. Every time she was around, his brain turned to mush and other parts of him hardened up.

She was the whole package. Cute. Sweet. Caring. Daring. Strong. Smart. Sexy.

And yet she was still grieving for someone he

couldn't compete with. It wasn't that he wanted her to forget Daniel; that wasn't even realistic. But he wanted a chance with her, and this weekend was his interview for the job of being her new boyfriend.

But she didn't need to know that.

He was going to woo her any way he knew how. For a brief moment, he thought about a singing telegram or a hot air balloon or maybe one of those planes that writes things in the sky.

Too much. Most definitely any of those would be too much.

Paige was easy to scare off. She was hardened on the outside sometimes, but soft on the inside. He had to take this slowly and hope that he could prove to her that she deserved to have love in her life again.

Love?

He couldn't think about that right now.

PAIGE WALKED OUTSIDE and took in a deep breath of the fresh air. Clover Lake had its own smell, full of grass and flowers and yeah, a little manure. But somehow it was a good smell. A clean, real life smell.

"Hey, girl," she said, working up her courage to reach her hand out to Noelle as she approached the fence. The horse was grazing but had walked to the fence out of curiosity when Paige approached. "You're a pretty girl."

"I bet she's thinking the same thing about you." She turned to see Brett behind her, smiling. He had changed clothes and was now wearing form hugging jeans, brown cowboy boots and a tight black t-shirt that showed off his muscular build. Why was her mouth watering so much?

"Hey. I didn't see you there. Just thought I'd take a little walk."

"She likes you," he said, pointing to Noelle.

"Oh yeah? And how can you tell?" Paige laughed.

"She never walks up to the fence like this. In fact, she's not a fan of strangers."

"I'm not a stranger. Am I, girl?" she said, rubbing the side of Noelle's face.

"Want to take a ride?" he asked.

Paige cleared her throat. "Sure. I guess you're going to make me ride my own horse this time?"

Brett looked down and then back up at her, a glint in his eye. "I'd rather you didn't."

"Oh. That's fine with me."

He climbed over the wooden fence and reached out for Paige. She put one boot - which she had remembered to bring - onto the wooden slat and he pulled her over.

The best part of getting on the horse was Brett putting his hand on her butt to push her up there. Now that she knew how to do it, she could probably get up there on her own, but there was no reason for him to know that.

As he slid in behind her, she felt the warmth of his legs around the outside of hers. It made her feel safe, which then immediately made her feel at risk. For loss. For heartbreak.

But she pushed those feelings away, somehow, and leaned back into him, allowing him to do all the work as she stared out over the open spaces.

Clover Lake was gorgeous. From its pastures to its thick woods to its small lake, it was like this oasis dropped into the middle of her desert of a life.

She was thirsty, dehydrated, but not for water. For love. She'd had it for an instant, and then it had slipped through her grasp. Daniel was the only one who had ever really loved her, including her biological family. His loss had changed so many things inside of her, not all good.

Her defenses were up, that much was sure. But when she was at Clover Lake - and with Brett - she felt like she could tackle anything. Take on the world. Take a risk.

Maybe fall in love again.

No, she couldn't think about things like that now. Her focus needed to be on laying Elda to rest, but a part of her felt like this weekend might also be about finally laying Daniel to rest. For real this time.

"WHAT IS THIS PLACE?" she asked as they came upon a small cleared piece of the property that she hadn't seen before. Brett slid off the horse and then reached up to help her off.

"This is where Elda's house stood."

Paige didn't speak for a moment and just looked at the Earth. This is where Elda grew up, played outside, spent her childhood years. She imagined her as a wide-eyed young girl, kicking a ball around the yard, not knowing that over ninety years stretched in front of her.

"I remember when we brought her here just after the house burned, before we cleared the charred remains away. She walked around and around this place, touching the remnants of her house. It was one of the saddest things I'd ever seen."

He spoke softly as they stood there, staring at the lush green grass surrounded by a battalion of tall trees.

"I can feel her here," Paige said, instinctively putting her arm around Brett's waist and resting her head on his upper arm. He stiffened for a moment under her touch and then slid his arm around her.

AFTER THEIR RIDE, Paige had a much better understanding of why Elda and Brett loved this place so much. It was like a world all its own, and she never wanted to leave. But she loved January Cove too.

For the first time in her life, she felt like she had more good in her life than she could handle. It was a strange sensation.

CHAPTER 11

*P*aige walked downstairs, following the smell coming from the kitchen. It was a mixture of apples and spices of some kind, and her mouth was watering at the aroma of it.

"What on Earth is that smell?" she asked with a smile as she saw Brett standing there wearing a "Kiss The Cook" apron.

"Aunt Elda's famous apple fritters. I thought we could have some for dessert." He looked down at the apron and laughed. "Like my apron?"

"I do," she said walking closer.

"Want to follow the instructions?" His tone was both playful and hopeful at the same time. She paused for a moment, actually considering the question. "I was just joking, Paige," he said with a chuckle before turning back around toward the counter.

Opportunity missed.

"So, what's the plan for tonight?" she asked, trying to will away the blush on her face before he saw it.

"Well, I was thinking we could have a picnic."

She furrowed her eyebrows in confusion. "Um... a nighttime picnic? It's starting to get dark out there already."

"But it's a clear, beautiful night. I have an idea if you're willing?"

She nodded. "Who am I to screw up anyone's idea?"

"Let's go then!" he said, walking around the breakfast bar and taking her hand. He picked up a real picnic basket - woven and all - as they went out the side door to the house. He walked to his truck, put the basket behind the passenger seat and helped her inside.

When he got in and cranked it up, she finally had to ask. "Okay, we're now in your truck. I thought we were picnicking here?"

"We are," he said, and then he didn't utter another word for several minutes until he pulled up at a clearing. They hadn't been to this part of the property together yet, but it was beautiful from what she could see. The edge of the creek poked out of the woods nearby, but it was mostly a clear spot, much like where Elda's house had once stood.

He stopped and walked around to open her door, helping her down into the lush green grass. She looked around, wondering where they'd be having a picnic since it was pitch black dark and there was no blanket anywhere in sight. Unless he'd shoved one in the picnic basket, they would be sitting on the grass which seemed awfully itchy and uncomfortable.

But this was Brett, and he always seemed to have a plan. He took her hand again - a new welcome feeling in her life - and led her to the back of the truck. "I'll help you up."

"Help me up? Into the back of the truck?"

"Trust me, Paige." She liked hearing those words coming from his mouth.

He stabilized her hand as she climbed up, and then he quickly followed her over with the basket in hand.

"Oh my gosh…" she said softly when she noticed that the back of the truck was filled with pillows and blankets. He had lined all sides with bright red pillows - from where she didn't know - and the bottom of the truck bed was cushioned with a couple of blankets and comforters. There was also a wooden bed tray that stood on four legs, and he was opening it as she watched. He pulled two large candles from the basket and lit them, his face finally illuminated under the night sky.

"Surprised?" he asked, his dimples catching the perfect light.

"I am. How'd you come up with this?"

"I guess you inspire me." He wasn't laughing. She wasn't either. "So, I hope you like sandwiches, because that's what I brought. I figured it'd be hard to eat much else in the dark in the back of a truck."

She smiled. "I love sandwiches. Ate a lot of them in my... traveling... days."

"I'd love to hear more about that sometime," he said softly as he handed her a wrapped sandwich and bag a potato chips. She reached into the basket and took a bottle of water.

"Not much to tell, really. It was a tough time of my life, but looking back I think it made me stronger."

"So it was worth it?" he asked, leaning back against one of the pillows.

She took a sip of her water. "I guess it was, not that I had much of a choice." Her pocket vibrated and she looked down to see Sandi calling. "Sorry about that," she said, pressing the decline button. Then she decided she didn't want to be bothered by anyone tonight, so she turned her phone off.

"If you need to take that…"

"I don't. It was just my friend Sandi back in New York. She knows where I am, but maybe she forgot. I'll talk to her tomorrow."

They continued to eat, with Paige regaling him with stories about her days as a gypsy, of sorts. He laughed at the funny ones, went serious at the stories that warranted that reaction. He seemed to hang on her every word, and that made her feel somewhat human again. Maybe she wouldn't always be "the mourning, grieving Paige". Maybe she could just be Paige again.

"So what about you? Any exciting things in your past, Brett Larson?" she asked as she leaned back against a pillow across from him.

"Compared to you, I think I'm pretty dull. Never sang on a street corner. Never worked as a puppeteer…"

Paige giggled. "I have a wide variety if skills."

"I bet you do." That comment made her whole body heat up.

"What about… women?" Why was she asking him this? It was really none of her business, but she was desperate to know how this handsome, smart cowboy was still single.

He sighed. "Not such a great track record there, I'm afraid."

Her stomach clenched. Just as she'd thought - something was wrong with him to be single this long.

"Oh."

"Not many women are suited for ranch life."

Her stomach loosened. "Really? This place seems like heaven on Earth to me. Of course, I've lived on the streets, under bridges and once in an airport bathroom for a weekend, so…"

"An airport bathroom?"

"Yeah, and let me tell you that it's hard to keep your feet up on the wall of a bathroom stall and sleep for very many hours."

Brett started laughing. "You are one interesting woman, Paige."

"So, no close calls? No marriage proposals?"

He became quiet and took a long drink of his water before answering. "I was engaged. About three years ago."

"Oh," she answered yet again. Conversation wasn't always her strong suit. "What happened?"

He sighed. "A lot of things, really. She thought

she wanted this life, but it turned out she wanted something else. Someone else, to be clear."

"I'm sorry, Brett."

He looked up at her, his eyes catching the light of the candles. "I'm not. If that had worked out, I wouldn't be sitting in the back of a pickup truck, eating dinner by candlelight with the most interesting and beautiful woman I've ever met."

Was it possible for a heart to literally explode? This was something she wished that she had researched before their dinner because hers was doing some kind of somersault-laden gymnastics routine in her chest.

"Thank you," she said softly, trying not to look at him now because there was a distinct possibility she might crawl across the blanket and kiss him so hard that his jaw broke.

"You have to get used to it, Paige."

"Used to what?" she said quietly after she finally looked up.

"I'm going to compliment you. I can't help it."

"Oh." She had to come up with a new word, but her language skills were escaping her at the moment.

HE THOUGHT IT WAS WORKING. Not that he was trying to play her or something. Everything he was saying was true, coming directly from his heart. He was putting himself out there like he never had before, and it was risky.

Still, she seemed to be enjoying herself. She was smiling a lot, laughing sometimes, asking questions. They had finished dinner at least an hour ago, and now they were lost in conversation about anything and everything.

Everything about being with her was easy. It was like his best friend in life had suddenly appeared from nowhere, and he didn't know how he'd ever survived without her.

But desperation wasn't cool on a guy. He couldn't come off that way even if he felt like she held onto the air that he breathed, and if she got up and left his whole world might come crashing down around him.

Right now she was talking about Daniel's family and how they treated her. Every time she spoke about Madeline Richmond, he wanted to drive his truck to New York and break his rule of never hitting a woman. He'd never do it, but the urge was definitely there.

"What about his other family?" Brett asked, trying to shake the violent feelings.

"He had a sister - Tori - and she was almost as bad as his mother. Her husband, Hampton, he wasn't as bad although when push came to shove, he'd stay on the Richmond side."

"Sounds like a wimp."

"Yeah, I think that's an appropriate word."

"So, can I ask you something without you getting mad at me?"

She laughed. "I can't promise that, but go ahead anyway."

She was honest; he'd give her that. "If this was the way his family treated you, what was your long-term plan?"

"What do you mean?"

"I see you as this strong and confident woman. I just can't imagine that you'd have taken her crap for very long. How did you think your future was going to look?"

She paused for a moment. "I guess I didn't really think that far into it. My life has been about moments. I had to survive one moment to the next, always on high alert. Daniel took that guard down, but I never really thought past that. He made promises that we'd travel and help people, so I assumed we would get away from them, I suppose."

Brett wasn't so sure about that. He never knew Daniel, but the idea of a rich man leaving his family behind forever didn't seem plausible, especially when he was working a family business.

But it didn't matter now.

"Come here," he said, motioning for her to slide to the center of the truck bed. She cocked her head sideways for a moment, but then she slid inward toward him.

He laid down, pulling two pillows behind him for both of their heads. She remained sitting up for a moment, but then slid down onto her back. There was barely air between them now, but he wasn't touching her or making any moves. Yet.

"Look," he said softly, willing himself to turn his eyes from her beautiful face and look instead up into the dark sky.

"Wow," she said, staring up at a sky full of bright stars. There was something to be said for country life. With no street lights to dampen the beauty, they could see the twinkling on full display. "That's amazing. I could never see this in the city."

"Did you see that? It was a shooting star," he said, pointing upward.

"I did! I've never seen one!" She was so excited, like a small child seeing everything for the first time.

"Make a wish."

"What?"

"You're supposed to wish upon a shooting star."

She turned her head and looked at him. "I can't."

"Why?"

"Because right now I have everything I want."

It was now or never. So he chose now.

He rolled to his left side and brushed his lips against hers. "Me too."

His lips were on hers, and she couldn't move for a moment. She wanted nothing more than to attack his lips with her own, but her body was betraying her.

"Paige? Are you okay?" he asked, his right thumb brushing across her cheek as he looked at her worriedly. "I'm sorry if I misread..."

"No, you didn't misread anything," she said with a slight smile. "I just surprised myself."

He pushed up onto his side a bit more, continuing to rub his thumb across her cheek. "How?"

"I thought I might freak out again, like I did at

the creek that day, but I'm not freaking out." She was full-on grinning now.

"You're not?" He matched her broad smile.

"Are you going to kiss me again soon or do I need to shut you up myself?"

"Feel free to shut me up…" he started to say, but her mouth was on his before he could get the words out.

And in an instant, they were entwined in the blankets, wrapped around each other and making some very nice new memories together.

WHEN THEY GOT BACK to the house, it was all Paige could do to wipe the smile off of her face. In fact, she'd been grinning so hard on the ride back that her cheeks literally hurt. But it'd been so worth it.

They had kissed until their lips were sore, and hers were about two sizes bigger than normal. And although they hadn't gone much further than kissing - he was a gentleman, after all - it had been more than enough.

She was a worldly woman, but not in that way. She had to love someone, know the relationship was going somewhere, before she gave up that part of herself. Otherwise, it was too scary.

But he hadn't asked. Hadn't pushed. Had held her close in his arms, made her feel safe out there in the middle of the dark wilderness. Took away every ounce of grief that was still pumping through her blood from months - actually, years - of pain in her life.

He just fit. They fit. It all felt so right, but still so scary. So tenuous, for some reason. Like the other shoe would eventually drop and she'd find out he was a serial killer or something.

He'd nuzzled the back of her head with his lips, his warm breath a constant reminder of his closeness as they laid there staring at the sky.

She'd seen what seemed like a hundred shooting stars, wishing on each one in her mind. Each wish a variation of the one before it - "Please let this be the one." "Please let this work out."

As they walked into the house, Paige noticed Elda's urn on the fireplace and stiffened. They were here for her, and yet she'd allowed herself to enjoy time with Brett. To feel something again. Maybe she was supposed to be feeling more grief and sadness, but somehow that didn't seem like what Elda would want.

"Now how about dessert?" Brett asked when they walked inside. His arms were around her waist from behind as he kissed up one side of her neck, his words muffled but understandable.

"What?" she asked, a little shocked at how forward he was being after remaining such a gentleman in the truck.

He dropped his hands and walked around her. "The apple fritters? I thought you wanted some? Or is it too late?" He craned his neck and looked at the clock which read 10pm.

Paige started laughing and put her right hand over her eyes. "Yes. Please. Fritters."

"Wait… Did you think I meant… *dessert*? As in you grab the whipped cream and I'll lick…"

"Stop! Don't finish that sentence," she said, giggling like an embarrassed middle schooler now. She sat down on the barstool and laid her forehead against the granite countertop.

Brett came up behind her and rubbed her shoulders. "Don't worry, Paige. I was just referring to the fritters."

She finally sat up, her face still flush, and watched him as he heated up two fritters and put them on plates. He climbed up onto the breakfast bar without warning.

"What are you doing?"

"Come on up. Let's be weird."

She climbed up onto the bar and sat cross legged across from him. "I think we've passed weird already. We had a night-time picnic in the bed of your truck, and now we're eating fritters on top of the kitchen counter."

"And you slept in an airport bathroom stall, so I'm just trying to catch up with you."

"True," she said with a laugh. It was funny that she found sharing her crazy stories with Brett made sense because she'd never told most of them to Daniel. The one time she'd tried - telling him one of her calmer tales - Daniel had looked at her in a way that made her clam up. She hated to think he was judging her, but it sure seemed that way.

"You know, I love hearing your stories." He took a bite of the fritter and wiped his hands on a kitchen towel.

"Oh yeah? Why is that?" she asked, leaning over and kissing him gently between bites.

"Because I want to know every part of you, Paige. And with every story, I get to meet another little sliver of who you really are. And I like every layer I get to uncover."

There was something slightly sensual in the way

he said it, even though she was pretty sure he didn't mean it to sound that way. She slid her plate and his out of the way and scooted forward, her legs placed around him. She felt his breath hitch for a moment before he put his hands on her butt and pulled her closer.

She put her mouth close to his without fully touching his lips. "I want to know everything about you too, Brett."

"You do?" he whispered back.

"I do. And I don't want to wait."

"Wait. What?" he asked, leaning back a bit and smiling at her.

"Life sometimes takes us places we don't expect to go. I've learned you can't count on tomorrow. You have to live for the moment. And in this moment, I want to be with you."

"Does that mean what I think it does?" he asked, clearly worried that he was misreading her intentions.

She pulled on his t-shirt and flipped it off over his head. "Is that clear enough?"

And more memories were made that night, but only after Paige made sure to cover Elda's urn with the kitchen towel.

CHAPTER 12

*B*rett woke up warmer than normal, but it was the kind of warmth that came from the inside out. For a moment, as the first glints of sunlight streamed into the room, he wondered if he'd accidentally ingested some drug that had made him hallucinate the best night of his life... because life couldn't possibly be this good.

He risked opening his eyes enough to see that the woman of his dreams was, in fact, cuddled against him, the back of her head resting just below his chin. Without moving, he could feel her backside pushed against his front side which was causing a cascade of physiological responses to happen already.

He could smell her hair - hints of strawberry mixed with vanilla and the scent of two bodies that had clung to each other for more hours than not in the last twelve hours or so. He could feel her breathing - relaxed, serene, peaceful.

"Are you smelling me?" she murmured as she slowly turned to face him. The satisfied smile on her face was a welcome sight.

"Maybe. Will you punish me if I say yes?" he said, playfully, kissing the tip of her nose.

"I'll consider it," she responded as she wrapped her free leg over his body and slid her free arm around his waist, pressing her cheek against his chest.

God, this was the most perfect morning ever.

"Can we just stay here forever?" she asked. It wasn't a joke; she truly seemed to be asking.

"You mean you don't want to go back to a small, dark bookstore with no customers?" Paige laughed at that.

"I love The Cove. It just needs some... updating. Revitalizing."

"Then let's do that. Let's make it just what you think it should be."

She pulled back a but and looked up at him. "Really? You'd trust me to do that?"

He smiled. "Of course I would. I'd trust you with anything, Paige."

She snuggled back into his chest, and he could feel her smile against his skin. This was going to be a good day.

PAIGE STOOD beside Brett at the creek. He was holding the urn with Elda's ashes and standing still, saying nothing. They'd been standing this way for ten minutes now, and she knew he was having a hard time figuring out what to say or do.

"You know, you don't have to say anything, Brett. You said it all at her memorial. You don't even have to spread her ashes yet. There's no rush."

He sighed and looked down. "This feels so final."

"If you're not ready, then let's not do it today."

Their morning had been spent enjoying each other in bed, eating a leisurely breakfast and finally getting into the golf cart to come to the creek. She knew he was procrastinating, and that part of it was knowing their weekend was over and they needed to go back to January Cove. Or at least she did.

"I miss her."

She slipped her arm around him and put her cheek on his chest. "I do too."

"Do you think she'd be happy about... us?" he asked.

"I think so. At least I hope she is."

She heard him swallow hard as he opened the urn. She stepped back, giving him the space she thought he needed, but as soon as he had it open, he pulled her close again.

"How good of a singer are you?" he asked.

"Terrible. Why?"

"I thought maybe some music would help it feel more official."

"I would only scare the wildlife, but let me use my phone." She pulled her phone from her pocket, but it was still turned off from the night before. She flipped it on, cleared the text messages quickly without reading them and found Amazing Grace on iTunes.

As soon as the song started, her eyes welled with tears as it always had when that song was played. And as he spread her ashes around the creek bed, Paige thought about the amazing grace that had brought her to Brett, and she silently thanked God for a second chance.

AFTER THEIR PRIVATE memorial for Elda, they headed back to January Cove. Paige was sad to see Clover Lake in the rearview mirror, but she was excited to be going home in a relationship with Brett.

Or were they in a relationship?

They hadn't really talked about it, but it appeared they were dating. She just didn't like to assume anything.

"So," Brett said as he pulled her close on her front porch. "Can I see you tonight?"

"Are you asking me on a real date, Brett Larson?"

He kissed her softly before he tipped his baseball cap. "Why, yes ma'am, I do believe I am." God, she loved his Southern accent.

She went up on her tip toes and kissed him on the cheek. "Then I accept."

"Pick you up at six?" he asked as he backed toward his truck. She nodded and smiled before turning to unlock her front door.

When Brett arrived at six, he was dressed in a nice pair of dark jeans, black lace up boots and a form-fitting gray t-shirt. She thought he looked good enough to eat, but she was too hungry to let that get the best of her. She needed some real food.

They drove to a new local restaurant called Onyx that sat just off the beach. It was a trendy place, built in a contemporary style with lots of large windows and steep angled architectural accents.

The place had one section with a bar that had loud music and a DJ, but they were eating in the fancier restaurant portion that overlooked the ocean. Amazingly, she could barely hear the music coming from the bar, and she marveled at the way they managed to keep the two separate.

The restaurant was beautiful with dim lighting, white tablecloths and a shiny, black grand piano in the corner. No one was playing the piano tonight, but the low jazz music piping through the restaurant made her feel like she was back in Manhattan.

"This place is amazing," she said as Brett pulled out her chair.

"Only the best for my Paige."

She loved how he said "MY Paige".

"You look stunning tonight, by the way. I toyed with the idea of pushing you right back inside your house and ordering a pizza so I could help you get out of that uncomfortable little dress."

She smiled. He had a way with words, but her stomach growled at just the mention of pizza. Or any food. She hadn't been to the grocery store lately, and she only realized that fact when she got home from Clover Lake.

"Thank you," she said "But I'm starving."

Brett laughed. "Then let's order."

They sat and chatted after ordering their food. Brett ordered lobster, and she ordered steak. The conversation was easy; the laughter was in large supply.

"So, my beautiful Paige," he said softly as he looked at her across the table, "I have something I want to ask you."

What? He couldn't be about to ask *that*. They hadn't known each other long enough.

"Um... Okay..." she stammered, unsure of what to say or do.

"Will you, Paige Emerson, my favorite person on Earth, do me the honor of... becoming my..."

Oh God. Oh God. What was she going to say? Why did she feel like saying yes no matter what he asked?

"Girlfriend?"

"What?"

"Will you officially take the title of girlfriend?" he asked. He was smiling broadly, completely oblivious to the fact that she'd just been having a mini panic attack inside of her own mind.

Girlfriend.

He hadn't asked for her hand in marriage. She

could breathe now. But why did she feel a little disappointed?

"Okay, you're making me nervous now. Don't you want to be my girlfriend?" Brett was looking at her, concern on his face.

Paige's heart restarted, sending a smile to her face. "Brett, I would love to be…"

"Paige? Oh my God, I found you!" a voice said from beside the table.

She didn't have to turn to know who it was, and then everything went dark.

PAIGE ATTEMPTED to open her eyes, but it was so bright. The last thing she remembered was the dim, elegant restaurant, so why was it so dang bright in here?

Was she in heaven? If so, she was happy to be there, but thought it sucked to have gone there so soon.

She tried again, but her eyelids felt like they had lead weights on them. She could faintly hear voices, some kind of conversation between a number of people, in the distance. It was low and rumbling and not at all understandable.

"Paige?" she finally heard a voice say. It was Brett. Someone was holding her hand. Actually, someone was holding both of her hands. But it didn't feel like the same person.

God, where was she?

Third time's a charm, she thought, as she attempted to open her eyes again. This time she was able to get them open and turned her head toward Brett's voice. He was looking down at her, his face filled with worry... and something else. Anger? Sadness? She couldn't tell.

"What... happened?" she managed to whisper. For some reason, she couldn't get her voice any louder.

"You fainted, sweetie," he said, rubbing her cheek with his thumb, something she was starting to like. A lot. She tried to reach up to touch his hand, but her hand was hurting. She looked down and noticed an IV in it, and then it started to make sense. She was in a hospital bed.

"I fainted? I've never fainted in my life." Now she was worried. And who was holding her other hand? She turned and then realized she was definitely hallucinating. Maybe they were giving her some kind of drugs. She whipped her head back toward Brett, tears in her eyes. "Something's wrong with me," she whispered. "I see Daniel's face. What medication have they given me?"

Brett closed his eyes and took in a deep breath.

"Paige, it *is* me, honey. I'm here. I'm alive." Daniel's voice. It was then that she remembered the last thing she saw before waking up in the hospital. It was Daniel, dressed in a black suit as he usually was, standing beside their table in the restaurant.

It was impossible.

She wouldn't turn her head back to him. Her heart raced and pounded so hard in her chest, that nurses came running again. And then they gave her something in her IV and she was out like a light yet again.

THE LOOK on her face had been pure torture for Brett. Seeing her expression at the realization that her fiance was alive made him want to scream. What did a person do in a situation like this?

He loved her.

There was no denying it anymore.

And if he wanted to be with her, he was now going to have to fight for her.

But should he? Wouldn't that be making her choose? Was that fair to her?

He loved her too much to have her always question if she made the right decision.

He wanted to throw up or punch somebody or scoop her up and run away with her.

Instead, he walked out into the hallway and then outside to get some air. The nurse said she'd be out at least another hour.

"Who are you?" Daniel said from behind Brett as he stood in the rooftop garden.

"I'm her boyfriend," Brett said, even though Paige never got to finish saying the words.

"Boyfriend. Wow. Okay…"

"Where the hell have you been? You faked your own death?" Brett turned and exploded in a barrage of accusations.

"Of course I didn't fake my own death! When I found out what my mother did, I was in rehab, trying like hell to get my speech back. Learning how to use a fork again. Learning to walk without a cane. I thought Paige abandoned me because I was damaged goods."

"She would never do that. You should've known that." Brett walked to the edge of the garden and looked out over the small town of January Cove, breathing in deeply in the hopes that the salty sea air would somehow make things better.

"As soon as I was able, I started looking for her. I've never stopped loving her."

There was a quiet between them. Brett struggled with being angry and feeling sorry for what Daniel had gone through. It was definitely one of those "rock and hard place" kind of moments.

"I think you should know that I intend to do everything in my power to take her back home to New York with me."

And there it was.

Brett turned and looked him in the eye. "Don't you think Paige should make that decision?"

"Look, I can give Paige the world. Traveling, contributing to her favorite causes, a life spent not wanting for anything. Do you really think this small town life is what she wants? Come on, man. You know she deserves better."

"That's where we agree," Brett said before turning to walk back inside. "She deserves better than either of us can ever give her."

PAIGE OPENED HER EYES, hoping that she was at home, warmly snuggled into her bed and not actually in the hospital. But when she heard the beeping of a heart monitor in the distance, she knew her situation hadn't changed.

And she knew there was a lot she had to deal with.

She looked around the room, but no one was there, so she pushed the button for the nurse.

"Miss Emerson, you're awake. How are you feeling?" the nurse said when she entered the room.

"Groggy and quite confused."

"That's to be expected. You've missed a whole day of your life," she said with a reassuring smile. "I'm Marlene, by the way."

"Nice to meet you. Is anyone here with me?"

"You have two gentleman in the waiting room," she said. For some reason, the thought of seeing either Brett or Daniel made her anxious. "And a young woman."

That part was confusing. Maybe it was Addison or Rebecca. "Do you know her name?"

"Sandra? Sandi maybe?"

"Sandi's here? Can you send her in?"

"And the men?"

"Not yet," Paige said, sending her a knowing smile.

Marlene walked out and came back with Sandi beside her, who promptly swooped in and hugged her friend tightly.

"Thank God you're okay!"

"I'm not sure I'd say that."

Sandi tilted her head and poked out her bottom lip. "I know this must be a lot to take in, sweetie."

She sat down in the chair next to Paige. "I don't understand how all of this happened. How is Daniel alive? How are you in January Cove?"

"I'll let him explain. I wish I could've gotten in touch with you this weekend. I was texting and calling, trying to tell you…"

"I turned off my phone."

"Yeah, probably not the best idea. When Daniel showed up at my apartment, I almost had a heart attack myself."

"Brett and I… we're…"

"He told me. I like him, Paige. He's a wonderful man."

"But Daniel…"

"Listen to me," Sandi said, leaning in to Paige's bedside. "You don't have to make any decisions right now. Take your time. Let's get you feeling better and then get you home. Then you can get the full story and decide what you want to do."

"You mean decide *who* I want."

Paige wanted to go back to sleep and let someone else make her decisions, but life just wasn't that easy.

CHAPTER 13

*P*aige was glad to be going home. Brett was driving her there, Sandi riding along in the backseat, but she still hadn't seen or spoken to Daniel again. She just hadn't been ready, but everyone in the truck knew that she was going to soon.

There was an air of discomfort around her no matter who was there. No one knew what to say, what to do. The whole thing reminded her of that Tom Hanks movie, Castaway, where the guy gets stranded on a deserted island and comes home years later to find his fiancee married to someone else.

Only she wasn't married to Brett. There was still time to make a choice between the two men, and it was a choice she didn't want to make.

Daniel was alive.

The thought made her so happy. He wasn't dead, still had a chance at a great life. Would it be with her? And if it was, what about Brett?

Her stomach flipped and flopped as they pulled into the driveway. Sandi would be staying with her for a few days, making sure she was feeling good. Even though the doctors weren't worried, Sandi most definitely was.

"I'll unlock the door," Sandi said, taking the keys from Paige as she got out of the truck.

Brett stood there, not overly close to her, obviously giving her space. He looked at the ground, fidgeted a bit more than usual.

"You need to talk to Daniel." There, it was out in the open.

"I know," she said, simply. What else was there to say?

"I can stay if you want…"

She looked up at him, a sad smile playing on her face. "No. It's okay. I think I need to do this alone."

Brett nodded, his face more serious than she'd ever seen. She knew he was looking for an answer, an assurance that she would choose to be with him, but she couldn't say that right now. Loyalties that were there before him couldn't just be wiped away that easily.

"I know this isn't easy, Paige. You make the choice that's right for you, okay? Somebody's going to get hurt either way you go, and I'm strong enough to handle it if that person is me."

"I don't want to hurt anyone," she said softly. He took her hands and brought them up to his mouth, kissing them softly.

"You deserve the world. Go with your heart, okay?"

She nodded, and he kissed her quickly on the cheek before turning and walking away without looking back.

She watched him drive off and then walked inside. Sandi was sitting on the sofa, looking as nervous as Paige did. Paige sat down beside her, leaned her head back against the sofa and sighed.

"When did you know?" she finally asked.

"A couple of days ago. Hampton tried to contact me first, about a week ago. I ignored his calls, assuming that the Richmond family wanted me to cater an event. I wanted nothing to do with that."

"Hampton?"

"Yeah. Apparently he left Tori. Couldn't stand it anymore, I guess. Spilled the beans to Daniel who was finishing inpatient rehab at a place in Connecticut."

"Wow. So Madeline whisked him off, told me he died and told him I abandoned him?"

"Seems that way."

Paige put her head on her knees and screamed. "God, why didn't I do more digging? Why didn't I go to the courthouse and look for a death certificate?"

"Who does that, Paige? You trusted the guy's mother to tell you that he passed away."

Paige stood and paced the room. "She put me through hell. She probably laughed so many times about how she got me. I hate her. I don't believe in hating people, but she's not even human."

"Agreed," Sandi said. "Listen, Daniel is on his way over. Do you want me to stay or…"

"I need to do this alone. But thank you."

Sandi walked toward the front door. "I'll take a nice long walk along the beach. Why don't you text me when you want me to come back?"

"Okay. Make sure to go by Jolt. It's a great coffee place."

Sandi nodded and closed the door behind her. Paige could feel the anxiety rising in her body, her hands sweaty, her heart racing.

And then she heard the knock at the door. When

she opened it, Daniel was standing there holding a bouquet of fresh, red roses - her favorite - and smiling.

"Hey, gorgeous," he said, with that perfect white smile. So familiar, yet so unfamiliar at the same time. Conflict raged in her gut.

"Come in," she said softly, stepping back and allowing him to enter.

She closed the door and put the roses in a vase on her side table before turning back to him. Daniel stepped forward and pulled her into a tight embrace, and she melted into a puddle.

Was it still love? Or was it relief?

"God, Paige, I missed you. I'm so sorry this happened. I thought you didn't want me..." She could hear his voice shaking, his own heart pounding as he held her close to him. He smelled the same - clean and sexy. He felt the same. But at the same time, nothing felt the same.

Tears streamed down her face. "I should've pushed harder to see you. I should've checked for a death certificate or something. I didn't know. I would've never left..."

He kissed the top of her head. "The good thing is we only lost a few months." She stilled.

Stepping back, she looked up at him. His eyes

were the same, but he had some small scars on his face from the accident. She noticed a slight limp when he walked, but otherwise he was the same Daniel who kissed her goodbye that morning.

And to him, it was time to pick right back up where they left off.

"Let's sit down," she said, pointing to the sofa. He held her hand and sat down right beside her, holding both of her hands in his and occasionally bringing them up to his mouth and kissing them. "You met Brett?"

Daniel took a deep breath and nodded, not making eye contact. "Do you love him?"

She hadn't been asked that question before. "I... don't know. It's new."

Daniel smiled slightly. "Paige, we aren't new. We have history. We had a life planned before..."

"Your mother."

"My accident."

They spoke at the same time. She chose to ignore their different answers for now.

"I want you to come home with me," Daniel said. It was part request, part demand, it seemed.

"Daniel, I can't just walk away from here. I have a job and friends and..."

"Brett?"

She paused for a moment. "Yes, and Brett. He certainly factors into the equation."

"Come on, Paige. You've known him, what, a few weeks? We were engaged! I have to say, I've been a little surprised - and let down - by your reaction to seeing me."

Frankly, she was surprised too. She loved Daniel. She always would. But seeing him had thrown a wrench in the new life she was starting to create for herself, and trying to imagine going back to New York was very difficult for her.

All she could think about was the blue waters of January Cove and the crisp spring breezes of Clover Lake. Nowhere in there were skyscrapers and pigeons.

She stood and walked to the kitchen, pouring herself a random glass of wine. She rarely drank, but right now she wanted to down the whole bottle.

"Paige?" he said softly from behind her. She didn't answer. "I love you. I never stopped loving you." She didn't turn around. "Are you still in love with me?"

Slowly, she took a sip of her wine and then turned. "If I'm being honest, I don't know."

Daniel's face looked like she had punched him in the gut. "Wow, I wasn't expecting *that*." He turned and walked back to the living room and sat down on the edge of the sofa, his elbows resting on his knees. "What changed, Paige?"

She sat down next to him on the sofa. "I grieved your loss for a long time. I didn't think it was possible to cry that much, to hurt so deeply that I literally wanted to curl up in a ball and die with you. I sat in that hospital waiting room, day after day, begging every member of your family to let me see you. To let you hear my voice. And then when your mother told me you died, I begged to come to the funeral." She shook as she spoke, anger and outright fury boiling under the surface.

"I'm so sorry, Paige. I had no idea. You have to believe me."

"I do believe you," she said, turning to look at him. His eyes were soft, welcoming, the same ones she'd planned to stare at each day for the rest of her life. Now, they were a source of confusion for her. Could she really let him go a second time? Not even give him a chance? Was he right about Brett? She had only known him a short time, but she had history - and life plans - with Daniel. Didn't he deserve something from her too?

It was all so confusing. And heartbreaking no matter which choice she made.

"There's something you need to know, Daniel."

"Okay…"

"Right before your accident, your mother came to a banquet hall where I was working and offered me any amount of money to leave you."

His face looked stunned, and he sighed audibly. But he said nothing about his mother.

"Please come back to New York with me. Give us a chance, a new start. Move in with me at the penthouse. We can start making our wedding plans again."

"It's not that easy, Daniel. It's just not. I can't just pick up where we left off like nothing happened. It wasn't either of our faults, but there are aftershocks." She stood and walked toward the front door, looking out the window at the ocean a couple of blocks over.

"Okay, I get it," he said, walking to her and putting his hands on her shoulders. "We can take it slow. Just come back to New York with me. You can stay at one of our hotels or get your own place. We can delay the wedding." He took her hand and then looked at her with confusion. "Where's your engagement ring?"

She swallowed hard. "I sold it to get the money to start over here."

His eyebrows shot up and he let go of her hand, stepping back. "Wow. Okay."

"I couldn't stay there, Daniel. Everywhere I looked, I saw the Richmond name."

"And that's so bad?"

"When it's connected with your mother and sister, yes."

He licked his lips and then bit the bottom one. "But you didn't want to remember me? Because I am a Richmond, Paige. And you will be too... hopefully one day soon."

The thought of becoming a Richmond made her feel queasy. And then she realized there was a question she had to ask - didn't want to ask.

"Daniel, did you cut ties with your mother and sister after you found out?" She stared into his eyes, waiting for an answer.

He swallowed hard and stepped back a bit more. He rubbed the back of his head, a move she had seen many times when he didn't want to have a confrontation with her about something, even as simple as where they would eat dinner. She could tell that the answer wasn't going to be a good one.

"They're my only family, Paige."

Knife.To.The.Heart.

"How could you?" she breathed out, only half able to form a coherent sentence.

"Paige…"

There was nothing he could ever say that would make it okay. She leaned against the front door. Tears streamed down her face while rage bubbled under the surface.

"There were so many times, sitting in that uncomfortable chair in the hospital waiting room, that I begged your mother for mercy. Begged Hamp to help me. Begged Tori, even. I tried everything I could, fell to pieces right there so many times. I was willing to do whatever it took to get to you, Daniel, because I was going to be your wife and I needed to be strong for you."

He walked forward and reached out in an attempt to put his hands on his upper arms, but she waved him off. "And I'm so grateful to you. I can't imagine what you went through. But now I'm here, and I want to be strong for you for the rest of our lives. I love you, baby."

Her eyes welled again and she shook her head. "No, Daniel. You had a choice. Maybe not a few months ago, but recently. You chose your mom and sister, which means I can't be your family." She opened the front door and stood there, stoically, not looking at him. In a rush, the scene with Brett and Amira in that very same living room played in her head. He had stood up for her, took care of her, gone to bat for her. Daniel had never done that. The reality of the fact that Daniel would've never cut ties with his mother for her set in, and it was a hard pill to swallow.

"Paige, come on, please. You know my family is complicated. We have businesses together. My Dad is gone and I'm the man of the..."

"She told me you were dead, Daniel. She put me through unimaginable hell, and yet you can forgive her. Let her stay in your life?"

"She got me through rehab. She was there for me when I had no one else. I can't just kick her out of my life now. She's my mother, for goodness sakes."

"Let me ask you a question," she said, staring up at him. "If I said I'd be with you but only if you moved here to January Cove, what would you say?"

He swallowed and looked away. "Paige, be reasonable." And there it was - she had never been worth it to him. She was a convenience, a way to irritate his family, a way to feel like he was a good person.

"Daniel, please go. And have a good life. I truly

mean that. But I won't be in it. Because this time, I choose *me*."

He walked past her and through the front door, but then turned swiftly and pulled her into his arms, planting a passionate kiss on her lips before she pushed his shoulders away.

"Stop!" she whispered loudly, trying not to catch the attention of her neighbors who were outside watering their lawn.

"I was hoping to change your mind." She stared straight ahead. "I can see that isn't going to happen."

"No. It's not." Her arms were crossed now as she watched him move down the walkway toward his rental car.

"You know, I was the innocent party in all this. I had the accident. I went through grueling rehab. I was lied to. And now I don't have you. Some redneck cowboy has you and what do I get?"

"Your mother," she said flatly before closing the door and closing that chapter of her life.

BRETT SAT in his car two blocks over and squeezed the steering wheel tightly.

"Ten…Nine…Eight…Seven…" he counted, a

method his father had once taught him for getting through angry moments without punching someone and getting arrested. Only there didn't seem to enough numbers to get him through this moment.

He wasn't a stalker, but he couldn't keep himself from parking out of sight and watching as Daniel arrived at Paige's house. He was there for over an hour, every minute ticking by like it was going through quicksand.

Brett imagined a passionate reunion with plenty of kissing and touching and...

He couldn't go there. His brain might actually explode.

He'd done the gallant thing and told her to choose with her heart and that he'd be okay. The only problem was that he didn't feel that way. He knew he wouldn't be okay with it.

And just when he'd convinced himself to drive away, go back to Elda's house at least, Daniel had appeared in the doorway with Paige.

And then they had kissed. The moment he saw their lips pressed together, he tore off down the road, his only aim to get away from that vision.

Now, a few miles down the road, he was struggling not to rip his steering wheel off and toss it into the ocean.

Dang it, why did he fall for her?

Just as he was getting ready to drive off again - this time to Clover Lake - he saw Sandi walking by. She was holding a coffee and checking texts on her phone.

"Hey!" she said as she passed his open window. There was nowhere to hide.

"Hey."

"I was just heading back to Paige's house. She said Daniel left. Mind giving me a lift?"

Brett shook his head. "Can't. Listen, tell Paige I wish her well, okay?"

"What?" Sandi looked completely confused.

"I saw her kiss Daniel. She chose him, and I can't stick around here waiting for my wedding invitation. Have a safe trip back to New York."

With that, he drove off toward Clover Lake vowing never to fall in love again.

CHAPTER 14

aige sat on the sofa of her small house and stared at the TV, which was turned off. She just needed something to stare at. Somewhere to turn her attention.

Finally, after what seemed like years, Sandi came through the front door. She looked worried.

"What happened? You're back with Daniel?" she asked, almost in more of a accusing tone. "Are you crazy? Brett is amazing. He's the one for you. I mean, Paige, listen..."

"Whoa whoa whoa!" Paige said, putting her hand up. "Take a breath. What're you talking about?"

"I ran into Brett down by the water. He saw you kiss Daniel."

"Oh no. I didn't kiss Daniel. I told him off and he grabbed me and kissed me."

"Well, Brett took off. He seemed very upset and told me to wish you well in your life back in New York."

"I'm not going back to New York." Paige frantically looked around for her purse and car keys. "I have to go."

"Paige, you can't drive! The doctor said for twenty-four hours…"

"Then you're driving me, but I'm not losing Brett. Let's go."

As they drove up to Clover Lake, the sun was starting to set with streaks of orange and pink in the sky.

"This place is amazing," Sandi said as she pulled down the dirt driveway. They made it halfway down the road before Paige saw his truck on the side of the road.

"Wait! Stop right here. Just stay in the car, okay?"

Sandi nodded, looking a little bit scared. She turned off Paige's car as Paige jumped out and ran into a thicket of woods.

She could hear the sound of the waterfall off in the distance, so she just ran toward it hoping to find Brett there. Her mind raced with worry, wondering if he was the type to do anything stupid when he was upset, but she brushed the thought away.

And then she saw him, standing on "their" rock, tossing rocks into the shallow water beneath. He looked sad and a bit lost.

She walked a little closer and stood there. "You know, it's not nice to watch people. It's a little stalker-ish."

He turned and almost smiled, but then the look faded.

"Why are you here, Paige?"

"You said I could come here anytime."

"You know what I mean."

She took a few steps toward him and stood just under the rock. He sat down, legs dangling over the edge of it toward her.

"This is my home, Brett. This place. You. January Cove. The whole mishmash."

His face registered some relief, but confusion lingered in his expression. "But I saw you kiss…"

"No. You saw him kiss me. Without warning or invitation. Out of desperation once I told him that it wasn't going to happen with us."

"You did?"

"Yes, I did," she said softly as she slid her hands across his thighs and stood between his strong legs.

"But I don't understand? You've certainly got a longer history with him, and he can offer you so much more than I can. You deserve the best, Paige. Even if that isn't me."

She reached up and touched his stubbly cheek. "He can't offer me lush green grass and waterfalls. He can't offer me a musty old bookstore. He can't offer me rides on horseback between a real cowboy's legs. He can't offer me night-time picnics with shooting star shows. And he sure as heck can't offer me homemade apple fritters and then countertop kisses with the chef."

Brett jumped off the rock and pulled her into a tight hug. "My God, I prayed you would come back, Paige. I wanted to fight for you, but I wanted you to be happy more than that. Just know that if any other dead boyfriends reappear from your past, I'm going to punch them."

She laughed. "Agreed."

"I don't believe I heard your answer at the restaurant. Will you please be my girlfriend?"

She smiled. "I would be honored to be your girlfriend, Brett Larson."

He looked down at her face and put his hands on both of her cheeks. "I love you, Paige."

"I love you too," she said.

And from the woods, they could hear Sandi giggling and saying "woo-hoo" under her breath.

This life was perfect.

CHECK out Rachel's other books at www. RachelHannaAuthor.com.

Made in United States
Orlando, FL
18 April 2024

45922095R00146